Toby Jones

——— AND THE ———
MAGIC CRICKET
ALMANACK

IT'S NOT JUST A GAME – IT'S TIME TRAVEL!

MICHAEL PANCKRIDGE

WITH BRETT LEE

Toby Jones

—— AND THE ——
MAGIC CRICKET ALMANACK

IT'S NOT JUST A GAME – IT'S TIME TRAVEL!

Angus&Robertson
An imprint of HarperCollins*Publishers*

All references to *Wisden Cricketers' Almanack* are by kind permission of John Wisden & Co. Ltd.

Angus&Robertson
An imprint of HarperCollins*Publishers*, Australia

First published in Australia in 2003
by HarperCollins*Publishers* Pty Limited
ABN 36 009 913 517
A member of the HarperCollins*Publishers* (Australia) Pty Limited Group
www.harpercollins.com.au

HarperCollins*Publishers*
25 Ryde Road, Pymble, Sydney NSW 2073, Australia
31 View Road, Glenfield, Auckland 10, New Zealand
77–85 Fulham Palace Road, London W6 8JB, United Kingdom
2 Bloor Street East, 20th floor, Toronto, Ontario M4W 1A8, Canada
10 East 53rd Street, New York, NY 10022, USA

National Library of Australia Cataloguing-in-Publication data:

Panckridge, Michael, 1962– .
    Toby Jones and the magic cricket almanack.
    For children aged ten to fourteen.
    ISBN 0 207 19982 5.
    1. Cricket – Juvenile fiction. I. Lee, Brett. II. Title.
A823.4

Cover photography by Alex Jennings; cricket memorabilia by Sport Memorabilia, Sydney Antique Centre
Cover design by Gayna Murphy, HarperCollins Design Studio
Typeset in 10/15pt Stone Serif by HarperCollins Design Studio
Printed and bound in Australia by Griffin Press on 80gsm Econoprint

5 4 3   04 05 06

To the wonderful game of cricket:
then, now and tomorrow.

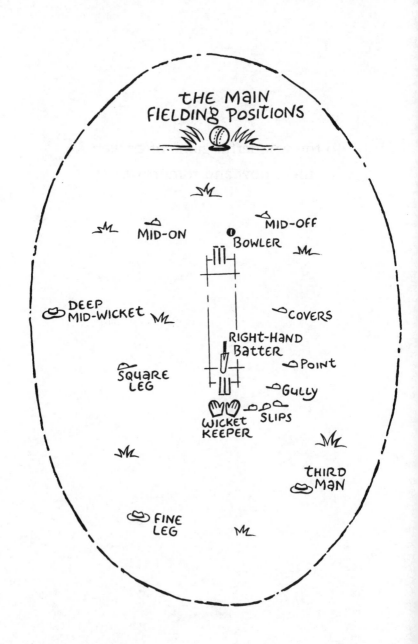

THE MAIN
FIELDING POSITIONS

MID-ON   BOWLER   MID-OFF

DEEP
MID-WICKET   COVERS

RIGHT-HAND
BATTER   POINT

SQUARE
LEG   GULLY

WICKET
KEEPER   SLIPS

THIRD
MAN

FINE
LEG

CLOSE UP OF
the CENTRE WICKET

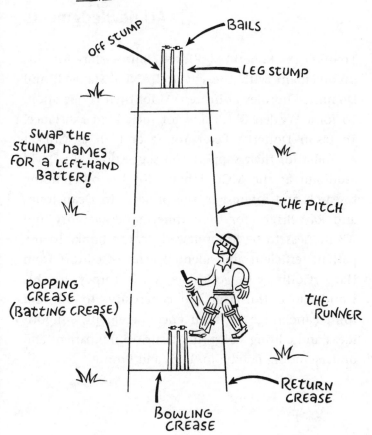

BAILS

OFF STUMP

LEG STUMP

SWAP THE
STUMP NAMES
FOR A LEFT-HAND
BATTER!

THE PITCH

POPPING
CREASE
(Batting crease)

THE
RUNNER

BOWLING
CREASE

RETURN
CREASE

Acknowledgments

Thanks to Robert McVicker Burmeister for his involvement with the cover. To Neil Maxwell and Dominic Thornley at Insite/ITM for their cooperation. To John Wisden & Co. Ltd for their kind assistance. To Jason Doherty, Peter Young and all at Cricket Australia for their support and suggestions. To David Studham at the MCC Library for his outstanding research and interest in the project. To Dean Jones and Ray Bright for their time, good memory and willingness to be 'interviewed' in the book. To the patient, efficient and talented team of editors from HarperCollins. To colleague Mark Torpey for his wonderful enthusiasm and generosity. To Bill and John Panckridge for their encouragement, support, ideas and editing skills. And lastly, to my patient and understanding family: Jo, Eliza and Bronte.

Contents

Foreword

JUST like Toby Jones, I was obsessed by the game of cricket when I was a kid. I was always looking for ways to improve my game. I learned so much from my older brother Shane, and from seeking the advice of coaches. I read every cricket book I could get my hands on and I watched and learned from my idol: Dennis Lillee. Dennis was my inspiration, someone who I looked up to. I wanted to be just like him. (As it turned out, he has had a lot to do with my cricket career.)

I am sure you will find that this book is not only an excellent read, but also a very useful guide to the game of cricket. It contains lots of great hints and information that I hope you will be able to use to improve your own game.

When I first became involved in cricket, I had no idea where the game would take me. The opportunities and possibilities it has created for me are endless. Cricket has taught me many valuable lessons. Most of all it has shown me that if I always play hard and *enjoy* the opportunity of representing my country, I will be successful.

Every time I get asked to offer cricket advice to kids, my answer is always the same: enjoyment is the most important part of the game. When I am on the field, you will nearly always find me with a huge smile on my face. After suffering several injuries in my younger years, I have learned to make the most of every moment I get to play cricket.

This book reminds me of my own childhood days spent in the backyard with my brothers, always battling hard on the pitch to see who would be the champion player at the end of the day.

Toby Jones and the Magic Cricket Almanack brings back truly great memories for me. I hope you enjoy reading this first book in the exciting new Toby Jones series.

Brett Lee

1 The Equation

Thursday — afternoon

'OKAY. Here's the equation. Listen up. Six balls to go. Nine runs to win. Can they do it? Jono, check your field. Toby, are you ready?' he said to me.

Mr Pasquali was excited. Boy, does he love his cricket. He is our cricket coach, and our class teacher too. Everyone wanted Mr Pasquali as their class teacher. Even the Year 3s were talking about him and hoping that they'd get put in his class when they got to Year 6. And if you were mad about cricket — like I was — then his class was the place to be. Mr Pasquali had a way of bringing cricket into most of the subjects we did.

It was the end of centre-wicket practice. We were tired, but Mr Pasquali always managed to keep us interested. Better still, I was batting. The only downer in the situation was the bowler, Scott Craven. He was fast, mean and ugly. Jono, our captain when we play against other schools, was going on the attack. He had two slips, a gully, third man, fine leg, then a ring of fielders

1

around me. If I could go over the top and score a two or maybe even a four (you hardly ever ran three on our small school cricket oval) then Jimbo and I just might score the nine runs we needed to win. Win what? Nothing, but still, getting one over Scott was something.

The first ball thumped into my pads. Scott yelled his appeal. Mr Pasquali had a good long look at me, then at my pads, and said firmly, 'Not out!'

Five balls left, still nine runs to get. Jimbo Temple strolled down the pitch.

'Toby, I'm running this ball, no matter what.'

You didn't argue with Jimbo. He was an awesome cricketer, but there was something about him that made you think twice before you spoke to him. He liked to keep to himself, and even Scott Craven kept pretty well clear of him.

I didn't see the next ball. It whacked me on the body. Jimbo was screaming at me to run. He was halfway down the pitch before I'd got my balance and set off. I felt clumsy and slow. My pads were flopping everywhere and my bat was heavy. And I had a throbbing pain in my ribs.

I hobbled up the pitch. WHACK! The ball smashed into my back. I groaned and stumbled on, finally making the crease at the other end. I really needed to work on my batting.

Once again Jimbo strolled up the wicket.

'Smart running, Toby. You saved your wicket. You okay?'

This was just about the most Jimbo had ever said

2

to me in one go. I was in pain, but Jimbo was on strike. What had I been imagining — putting Scott away for a four?

'You're history, loser,' Scott sneered at Jimbo as he walked past us.

Jimbo didn't seem to notice. 'Back up, and listen for the call, okay?'

I nodded.

Jimbo strolled back, took a look at the field, which hadn't changed, then settled down to wait for Scott. The boys in the field were clapping and urging the bowler on.

Scott raced in and sent down a thunderbolt. It was a beamer. A massive full toss heading straight for Jimbo's head. He ducked out of the way, just, as the ball flew past him. It was too hot for Martian — Ivan (Ivo) Marshall, the keeper. The ball bobbled down towards fine leg. Jimbo looked at me. I can't have looked too keen. He held up a hand and shouted, 'No!'

'You're a wimp, Toby Jones. Gutless wonder,' Scott sneered at me as he walked past.

'Okay. It's going to be tough,' yelled Mr Pasquali. 'Four balls to go, seven runs to win.'

'Hang on. What do you mean four balls? I've bowled three already.'

Scott Craven was looking mean. He knew the answer.

'That last ball was a no ball, Scott. Extra delivery and a run to the batting team. If you're good enough you should win it from here. Look alive, everyone!'

Jimbo tapped his bat on the crease and waited. He looked as calm as ever. Scott started his run-up. He was actually a very good bowler.

Suddenly there was a mighty THWACK. I almost missed it. One minute Jimbo was tapping his bat in the crease, the next he was leaning back, bat high in the air, watching the ball sail over covers and out towards some sheds near the school fence.

'Hey, Jay. Did that clear the line?' Mr Pasquali called.

Tough call for Jay, but he was in the best position to judge. He nodded.

'I think so,' he shouted, then jogged off to get the ball from up against an old hockey goal.

Scott Craven was fuming. In one shot, Jimbo had reduced the equation to three balls and one run. We were level.

'Control and focus,' Mr Pasquali was saying to everyone. 'Each of you, think of your role here.'

Jono was bringing all the fielders in close to the wicket.

'Good thinking, Jono. No good having anyone out now. You've got to stop the single,' Mr Pasquali said.

I looked at Jimbo. His expression hadn't changed. There was no excitement on account of his six. We hadn't won yet.

I turned round to look at Scott Craven. He was waiting at the top of his run-up, looking down at the ball. He was changing his grip. Being a bowler helped me know about these things. He was going to bowl a 'slow' ball. You know, when everything looks the same: run in just as fast, and then out it comes — slow — either through the back of the hand, or with a finger tucked behind so it doesn't come out with all the power it should.

Jimbo played all round it. He completely missed the ball. It made him look clumsy, but luckily the ball was wide of the stumps.

'Two balls, one run,' bellowed Mr Pasquali. He didn't need to. Everyone knew.

Scott's next ball was probably his best of the over. A fast yorker. Jimbo just managed to get a bit of bottom edge onto it, which was just as well: otherwise he would have been lbw.

Now everyone was tense. Scott Craven was talking with Jono Reilly at mid-off, nodding his head. I looked at Jimbo and started walking towards him.

'I can tell if it's a slow ball. I'll raise my bat if he's going to bowl it.'

Jimbo looked at me. 'Good idea, Toby. Then get ready to run.'

I had a job to do, but I didn't want to make it too obvious. I turned away from Jimbo and looked out past Mr Pasquali to where Scott was standing.

'Okay everyone. This is it. I want a winner here,' called Mr Pasquali.

Scott hadn't looked down at his hands. He started to move in. I stared at his bowling hand, desperately trying to see his grip. He was halfway in now, almost at full speed. Suddenly his other hand shot down to the ball. He was changing his grip. I pushed my bat up into the air as Scott approached the bowling crease. I just hoped like anything that this was going to work.

Scott swung his arm over and let go. Jimbo waited. The ball seemed to take ages to get to him. Jimbo stepped back, but the ball was bang on line, heading for middle stump. He pushed at it with all his force, looking for the gap between bowler and mid-off.

'Yep!' he shouted, as Scott dived towards the ball. I took off. A moment later I heard a yell from behind. Scott had grabbed the ball and flicked it at the stumps. Everyone looked at Mr Pasquali, who was staring at the broken wicket.

He pointed both his hands up to the sky and drew a box in the air. He was asking for the third umpire, the way they do in cricket matches on TV. Jimbo had kept on going, not even interested in the result.

'Too close to call that one, boys. Great finish though.'

'I thought you wanted a winner?' said Scott Craven. He looked tired.

'You're all winners today,' Mr Pasquali beamed. 'Now let's get this gear packed up. And don't forget that tomorrow some of you are coming on the excursion to top all excursions: the MCG visit.'

As if any of us could forget that. I couldn't wait!

Thursday — evening

At the dinner table, I told Mum and Dad about cricket practice. They were always interested to hear how

6

practice went — I reckoned Dad was sometimes more interested in cricket than he was in any of my school subjects. Even Natalie, my eight-year-old younger sister, was tuning in.

'Anyway, you can bowl faster than Scott Craven can't you, Toby?'

'Of course I can, Nat. I can bowl faster than Brett Lee!'

'And I've climbed Mount Everest in a kilt,' Dad said, ruffling my hair.

'Well, I might bowl as fast as him one day.'

Mum looked across at me. 'Yes, Toby, one day you just might.'

Practice — Make it like a match

Taking the opportunity to simulate match conditions during your practice sessions is a great way to give players some experience. You can never totally re-create real game situations, but putting batters, bowlers and fielders under stress is a good way to see who can stand up and perform under pressure.

Turning practice into a game situation also adds interest to the practice. It gives the players something to focus on. Most players love a bit of competition, and most players love to win.

Near the end of a long practice session, introducing a game element, like setting a target to chase, creates the chance for someone to be the hero, if only for a few moments before everyone wanders away to pack up and head home.

The best bowling figures in a World Cup match are held by Glenn McGrath of Australia. He achieved figures of 7/15, against Namibia, during the 2003 World Cup. Two other bowlers have taken seven wickets in a World Cup game. They are Australia's Andy Bichel (7/20) and the West Indies' Winston Davis (7/51).

2 The Library

Friday — morning

THE next morning I was up early. It was the day of the excursion to the MCG — *the* Melbourne Cricket Ground! You could choose to go to other places, but any chance to get to the MCG — and with Mr Pasquali as well — was something you didn't knock back. My best friend, Jay Bromley, felt the same. He'd never been there, but he'd heard me talking about it often enough.

There were 10 of us going from my year — all boys, except for Georgie — plus Mr Pasquali and Jono's dad, Mr Reilly. Georgie loves sport, and it didn't bother her that she was the only girl taking the MCG tour.

Georgie was great. She lived with her mum at the other end of our street, and we'd played together since we could walk. Our house was like a second home for her. Often Georgie's mum would call round and end up staying for dinner. Georgie and I, and

9

sometimes Nat, would play cricket outside, or down the hallway if it was dark.

Most of the cricket team were going on the tour except for Jimbo, who was doing the Old Melbourne Gaol. Jimbo was different, somehow. He was friendly if you spoke to him, but he didn't seem to be too interested in being with other kids. Georgie said that the opposite was actually the truth, that he really wanted people around him. I wasn't so sure. There was something about him that I liked all the same.

Anyway, Mr Pasquali, Jono and his dad, Jay, Rahul, Martian, Cameron, Minh, Georgie and I, as well as Scott Craven and his best mate Gavin Bourke, were taking the tour from heaven.

When we arrived at the MCG we passed through a modern front section with lots of glass and then went through an older-looking gate. This was the back of one of the big stands, which we walked around underneath.

Jay was looking pretty impressed, but he really wanted to get out to the actual ground, which we kept getting little glimpses of. He wasn't really listening to the stuff we were being told about the dressing rooms and other places.

They took us upstairs past some fantastic pictures of old players; they were massive. I kept thinking how much Dad would have loved this. It was sort of like a museum.

Then we came to a little library, stacked with books — all on cricket. The floor creaked as we moved quietly into the room. It was cluttered and busy. There were piles of books on tables and on the floor. The place was messy, but you got the feeling that this was how it was meant to be. There was a heap of brown and yellow books in a bookshelf just on the right.

'*Wisden Cricketers' Almanack*s,' said a small voice behind me. I jumped. An old man with a wrinkled face and a kind smile was looking at me. 'Would you like to see one?' he asked.

I looked across at Jay. He shrugged.

'Um, yeah, okay. Thanks,' I replied.

The old man unlocked a glass door and pulled down one of the brown books. It had '1949' in gold letters on its thick spine.

'Have you heard of the Invincibles?' the man asked me. His eyes were sparkling.

'Wasn't that Sir Donald Bradman's team?'

'He was part of the team, yes, and other great players too. Go on, open it.'

I must have been holding the book as if it was some kind of treasure, too afraid to open it and turn the old, musty-smelling pages. The rest of the group were leaving the library, but I couldn't put the book down. It felt so warm and comfortable in my hand.

The nice old guy was smiling. 'My name is Jim Oldfield — and do call me Jim, boys,' he said. 'I was wondering, would you mind opening the book and telling me what you see?'

'C'mon, Toby,' called Jono's dad from the library door.

It was as if a spell had been broken.

'Coming, Mr Reilly,' I said reluctantly. 'Mr Oldfield — er, Jim — was just showing me these old books.'

'You want to stay on a bit? We're just heading out onto the ground,' Mr Reilly said.

'Yeah, okay. I'll catch up with you soon. See ya, Jay.'

I looked over at Jim's friendly face then back down at the book I was holding in my hands. Jim was nodding at me, urging me to open the book.

My first reaction was that there must be something wrong with my eyes. Maybe they had dust in them. There was probably plenty of that floating around an old room like a library. Everything on the page — the words and numbers — was blurry and shimmery, as if it was in water. The words kept dissolving, then reappearing. I closed my eyes and shook my head. Then I looked back at the open book in my hands. It was the same again.

'See if you can find page 221,' Jim suggested.

It was so weird. 'What's going on?' I stammered. 'I can't read this.'

There was a pile of different cricket books on the oval table where old Jim was sitting. He pushed one towards me.

'You open it,' I said.

He smiled and did so.

We both stared at the open page. Everything looked normal. There were no swimming words. I grabbed another book and flung it open. It was the same. I squeezed my eyes shut again.

There was something about the old brown book. I turned it over in my hands, peering at the sides and the spine, trying to work out how the blurry effect was achieved.

'Toby,' said the old man, 'page 221. Go on.'

'Are you coming, Toby?' It was Jay, standing at the door of the library. He must have come back to find out what had happened to me.

'Jay ... come over here and look at this wisdom book.'

'*Wisden* book, Toby. *Wisden*.'

Jay was looking a bit surprised. He glanced over at me with a questioning sort of look. I was glad I hadn't told him what I'd seen. I was wondering whether the book would have the same effect on him.

Jim passed Jay the book.

'Is there a famous cricket match in here or something?' asked Jay, sitting down and opening the book at its first page.

'Try page 221,' I suggested.

Jim sat there, nodding his head.

Jay flicked through the pages fast, then stopped turning, presumably at page 221. I sat down next to him.

Jim was staring at me, almost sadly. Then his eyes went to the book. 'Read it, Jay,' he said.

'He probably won't be able to,' I offered, my eyes finding their way back to the page.

'What do you mean, "won't be able to"?' scoffed Jay, and he started to read.

13

'"Essex v Australians. At Southend, May 15, 17. Australians won by an innings and 451 runs. In light-hearted vein, they made history by putting together the highest total ..."'

Jim was chuckling, the wrinkles on his face crinkling like cracks in dry mud. His chuckles turned to coughs.

Jay looked up from his reading. 'What's the joke, then?'

'Tell him, Toby. Tell Jay here what you see when you open the *Wisden*.' Jim was speaking softly, his voice a bit raspy.

I picked up the book yet again and opened it. The letters were a blur. Now and again vague shadows would appear, then just as quickly they would vanish into the white mist of the page. I pushed the book towards Jay, who was looking at me oddly.

'Jay,' I said, 'can you really see the stuff on this page here?' I pointed at the page. I even touched it. It felt warm and alive, like the book had when I'd held it.

By now, I knew that Jay sensed something was up. 'Is it your eyes or something?' he asked me.

'Close the book and look at me. Both of you.' Jim was speaking softly but firmly. 'There is nothing wrong with you, Toby. On the contrary, we have discovered that there is something quite special about you. If you give me five minutes, I can explain exactly what I mean.'

Jay and I looked at each other. He shrugged and

said, 'You tell me later, Toby. I'm heading back to the group.'

Jim stood up and made his way over to the glass bookcase where all the heavy brown and yellow books stood. He reached in and took down another *Wisden*. It looked even older than the one lying on the table in front of us.

'You see, Toby, you and I share a special gift. These pages are the doors to cricket matches from the past. It's a funny thing, but I knew that you would eventually arrive here in the library. That's the thing about time travel — you learn all sorts of things about the future that you normally wouldn't know.

'Let me explain. In 1930 I was nine years old and living in Leeds, in England. Don Bradman was touring with the Australians. My father had bought tickets for both of us to go to the first day's play. But the night before the match, I became very ill; I'm afraid I deteriorated so badly that by the time Don Bradman walked out to bat on that second day, I was lying in a hospital bed.

'I missed one of the most remarkable innings ever played in the history of Test cricket. Instead of marvelling at the greatest batsman anyone will ever see, I lay on a hospital bed fighting for my life.

'Well, as you can see, I survived the illness. But six months before the Second World War started, my father died quite suddenly. My mother and I came out to Australia and she let me bring my father's collection of *Wisdens*, all 11 of them.'

I had a thousand questions flying through my brain, but Jim raised a finger to his lips as I was about to speak.

'Now that I'm an old man my powers have weakened and I can't travel, without the help of someone else who has the gift,' he explained. 'And even with you here now, Toby, and even if you were willing to help an old man like me, I fear that my time for travels of this kind are well behind me. Alas, that match of 1930 will remain a dream. As it always has been. You see, I have a memory of six words that I have played and repeated in my head all these years. "Don't ever come back here alone." I took it to mean don't come back to the time of 1930 alone. I don't remember who said the words to me. My father? Perhaps my grandfather. Anyway, I have obeyed the instruction.' Jim looked away for a moment. 'But you, Toby, with my help, have the opportunity to, to ...'

I swallowed.

'To travel back through time. To watch any game you choose. To ...'

There was a noise behind me. The wall opened and a lady walked in with a plate of food. I jumped.

Jim chuckled and said, 'This library is full of surprises.'

'Jim's spinning his stories to you, is he?' the lady asked cheerfully, setting a plate of sandwiches down in front of him. She headed out again, but left the door open. I bounced up and looked at it, checking

16

both sides. From the inside it looked like a solid wall, but there was a handle on the other side.

'Alas, I fear the spell has been broken,' Jim said quietly.

I went back to my chair and stood behind it.

'Here, Toby. Take this.' Jim had pulled a small sheet of paper out of his shirt pocket and passed it over to me.

'That's my father's handwriting. He copied it from a letter that his father wrote to him.'

I took the sheet from him, and without looking at what was written on it, slid it into my shirt pocket.

'Come back will you? Sometime?'

I walked over to the door. 'Thanks for the story and all that, Jim.' I turned towards him but was afraid to make eye contact.

Jim didn't reply.

The first catch taken by a substitute in Test cricket was an odd affair. In 1884, the Australian captain, Billy Murdoch, came on to field for England as a substitute. He caught his own team-mate, who had top scored with 75. The injured English player was W.G. Grace.

3 The Chase

FOR the rest of the excursion I was in a daze.

'You're quiet, Toby,' someone was saying to me.

'Huh?'

It was Georgie. 'I said ...'

'Yeah, I know.'

'He's been freaked out by an old guy in that library,' said Jay.

'Well?' she was looking at me, expectantly. Georgie never missed out on anything.

'I'll tell you later,' I said.

'Before he dies. Promise?' she chuckled.

I must have looked a bit shocked.

'Just joking!'

The sheets of paper on my clipboard stayed blank. It wasn't till I was on the bus, sitting next to Jay, who had three or four pages of notes and sketches, that I reached into my pocket and pulled out the piece of paper that Jim had given me.

When Jay looked over and asked me what I was reading, I filled him in.

'Why don't you just chuck it away and forget about it?' he said, watching me scan the words in front of me.

I didn't answer. It was as if the words were talking to me. There was no washy effect with these words. They were clear and still on the paper.

> *What wonders abound, dear boy, don't fear*
> *These shimmering pages, never clear.*
> *Choose your year, the* Wisden *name,*
> *Find the page, your destined game,*
> *Then find yourself a quiet place*
> *Where shadows lurk, to hide your trace.*
>
> *Whisper clear date, place or score*
> *While staring, smitten; then before*
> *(You hope) the close of play,*
> *Be careful now, you've found the way.*
> *So hide your home, your age, your soul*
> *To roam this place and seek your goal.*
>
> *Be aware that time moves on —*
> *Your time, this time; none short, or long.*
> *So say aloud two lines from here*
> *Just loud enough for you to hear.*
> *From a quiet spot, alone, unknown,*
> *Back through time, now come — alone.*

And never speak and never boast,
And never taunt, nor ever toast
This knowledge from your time you bring.
To woo the rest, their praises sing:
They wonder, and your star shines bright ...
Just this once, this one short night?

But every word that boasts ahead
Means lives unhinged, broken, dead.
Don't meddle, talk, nor interfere
With the lives of those you venture near.
Respect this gift. Stay calm, stay clever,
And let the years live on forever.

Dear Jim,
'Tis all, perhaps, for another time ...
Your loving father,
Ernest James Oldfield

For a few minutes I stared at the words, trying to work out their meaning. I was a bit spooked by the unhinged, broken, dead part. I thought of showing Jay, but he was talking to Martian across the aisle. Somehow, these old words from another time didn't seem right. I was also afraid that Jay would convince me that all this time travel stuff was stupid. I didn't want that. There was something exciting happening here. I wanted to explore it further. Maybe I'd show Georgie. She was really smart. She'd know what it all meant.

The most exciting thing about the last two days of the school week was the announcement of the cricket team for our first match of the season.

Jimbo hadn't been selected. None of us could work out why, because he was probably the best batsman in the school.

'There's a reason for everything,' Georgie said, shaking her head as she looked at the team sheet outside the gym. 'But I sure would like to know the reason for Jimbo not playing tomorrow.'

'He's lazy, that's why.' Scott Craven had come over to add his thoughts to the conversation. 'He's not a team player. I reckon Mr Pasquali's giving him an ultimatum. Play for the team or you're not gonna be a part of it.'

I wasn't about to start arguing with Scott — even if his reasons were wrong. That's what he was waiting for. Scott Craven was forever looking for a reason to start an argument.

I looked again at the team sheet. All the familiar names were there. Cameron and Jono, our openers. Rahul, Jay, Scott, myself and Gavin and Georgie. Then Martian, our keeper, and finally Minh and Ahmazru. I didn't think it was the batting order, but it wouldn't be a bad one if it were.

Saturday — morning

I pulled my hands out of my pockets, rubbed them together, then turned to watch Scott Craven run in to bowl the first ball of our first game of the season.

21

We were playing Motherwell State School. There were six teams in our competition for this season. Our team was Riverwall. The other teams were St Mary's, TCC, Benchley Park and the Scorpions. Everyone was talking about the Scorpions and their players. They were new to the competition and not much was known about them. But their name was different, and the rumours were that they were a tough, strong and talented group of cricketers.

The ball thudded into the batsman's pads. The batter buckled over, and amid the shouts looked up at the umpire. Slowly the umpire raised his finger.

'Yeah!' shouted Scott, and he pumped both fists in the air.

The cricket season had started.

Scott Craven was awesome. In many ways it wasn't fair that he was playing school cricket. He was so good he probably should have been playing with older kids. We had two amazing cricketers — Scott Craven, our fast bowler, and Jono Reilly, one of the opening batsmen. Without them, we would have been an average team, winning only some of our games. With them, I reckon we were pretty well unbeatable. There was a third great player — Jimbo. I just hoped that I'd get to see him play in a real game.

It was lucky for the opposition that you could only bowl 5 overs and had to retire at 40 runs.

None of us really liked Scott Craven, or, for that matter, Gavin Bourke, his best friend. But we were glad to have him on our team. Scott was loud, confident and extremely short-tempered. He could be quite mean with his comments to us, and we usually got a spray from him if one of us dropped a catch from his bowling.

Scott took another wicket in his next over, clean bowling the batsman and sending the off-stump cartwheeling back towards Martian, our wicket keeper.

I was used as a first-change bowler. Sometimes I opened, but I think Mr Pasquali liked to give the opposition a break from having to face two fast bowlers first up.

I wasn't as quick as Scott, though I didn't try for flat-out pace. I was working on swinging the ball through the air and trying to perfect a slower delivery.

My first ball was a full-length delivery outside off-stump. The batsman took a swing at it and missed. I repeated the delivery with my next ball, but this time put it out a fraction wider. Again the batter went for the ball, and this time it caught the edge of his bat and flew through to Martian. He took a neat catch in front of Jono at first slip.

My other wicket came in my third over. It was an attempted slower ball that would have been called a wide. But the batter reached out for it and flat-batted it out to cover. Scott Craven took the catch.

Scott picked up another 2 wickets himself to add to his earlier 2.

Cameron, Georgie and Jono each got 1 wicket. The last wicket was a run-out. We ended up having to score 109 runs to win. Mr Pasquali must have been confident, because he changed the batting line-up. Martian was pushed down to number seven, my normal spot, and I went up to number four.

Jono and Cameron put on 47 runs before Cameron was bowled. I got my first bat of the season after Rahul was run out for only 5. He had lost his glasses halfway up the pitch and for a moment it looked as if he was going to stop and pick them up.

Jono and I put on another 30 runs before Jono was caught on the boundary for 33. By then we had scored 88 and the game was as good as over. Jay strode out to the wicket. He normally batted further down the order, too.

Mr Pasquali retired me on 25 not out. Gavin came in and left almost as quickly, clean-bowled for a duck. Then Scott Craven blasted two sixes to win the game for us.

We batted on until we'd faced the same number of overs we had bowled. You got bonus points for batting and for bowling — a point for every 30 runs and for every 2 wickets. We ended up making 164. I couldn't wait to check the paper to see how the other teams had gone.

It was a good first-up win. Nothing spectacular, as Mr Pasquali said, just a solid all-round team performance.

After the game I asked Georgie what she was doing that afternoon, and when she said nothing, I said I'd get online at about four o'clock, as I had some news for her. I wanted to tell her about my conversation with Jim at the Melbourne Cricket Club library, and I particularly wanted to show her the poem that Jim had given me. She'd take that seriously, even if she didn't believe anything else I said.

We liked to chat online and had made a chatroom for ourselves last year, when we'd first started playing together in the same team. We called it CROC — Cricketer's Room of Chat. It was a bit like a secret club, I suppose, but cricket was the general theme. I suppose we could have just used the phone, but somehow it was more fun chatting over the Internet. The other bonus was that suddenly Jay or Rahul or Martian could jump in and join the conversation.

I logged on just before four o'clock. Georgie was the only person logged into the room.

Georgie: so, what's news?
Toby: maybe i sh have told you earlier ... you rem. the old guy in the lib at the mcg?
Georgie: yeah.
Toby: well, this'll sound v stupid but i think i have this gift that makes me able to travel in time. georgie, you there?
Toby: hey! georgie ...
Georgie: yeah, i'm here. toby?
Toby: yeah.
Georgie: you're an idiot!
Toby: i know. but it's true.

Georgie:	are we going to keep on with this, cos i've got better things to do.
Toby:	wait. i've got a poem for you.
Georgie:	that sounds better. when did you write it?
Toby:	i didn't. but you'll like it. scanning now.

I pulled the piece of paper out of my desk drawer, and, keeping it in its plastic pocket, placed it on the scanner. A moment later I was waiting for Georgie to accept the file I was about to send.

| Toby: | what do you think? georgie? |

But that was the last I heard from her. She was either totally sick of the whole idea of time travel, or else of reading the poem and trying to work out just what the heck it meant. I guessed I'd find out. Eventually.

I caught up with Georgie at recess the following Monday.

'Interesting poem, Toby. Where'd you get it?'

I explained everything to her, not leaving out any details. It was actually good to say it all out loud. She listened carefully, without interrupting.

'That's it?' she said, when I had finished.

'So far, yes.'

She looked at me for a moment. Slowly a smile spread across her face.

'Like I said, great poem. Can I keep it?'

'Of course. But what about the rest? You know, the *Wisden* cricket book stuff? The wishy-washy writing?'

'Well, go back to the MCG and do it. That's the only way to prove anything.'

'You don't believe me, do you?' I asked her.

'I believe *you*, Toby, but I sure don't believe anything else.'

'Meaning?'

'Meaning that I don't think you would make up all this to trick me, but I think someone else has made it all up to trick you.'

Georgie sure had good logic. You could never argue with her. About anything.

'Okay, maybe you're right,' I said. 'Will you come with me next time I go?'

'What, to the library?'

'Yeah. You can meet Jim yourself.'

'Okay, but I won't hold my breath or anything.'

'Cool. Hey, did you book the gym for lunchtime tomorrow?'

'Yep. And I'm bringing a friend, too.'

'Who?' I asked.

'You'll see,' she said mysteriously, and then turned and headed off towards a group of kids near the playground.

Monday — afternoon

The great thing about having Mr Pasquali as our teacher was that he let you do a sport project of your choice. For this one we could just concentrate on cricket. Later in the year we could do another cricket project, but that one would have to have a history and culture theme.

After school that day, Rahul and Jay came around so we could work on our projects together.

Rahul was doing the Tied Test that happened way back in 1986 between India and Australia. Being Indian himself, Rahul was pumped to be working on something so close to his heart. It was close to his family too. They came from Madras (now called Chennai), the place where the match was played, and migrated to Australia not long after it took place.

I was doing my assignment on the 1999 cricket World Cup. Jay had finally decided to study Don Bradman. He had changed his mind about four times.

Even Craven was putting in a huge effort. He was doing the Bodyline series, and was using a computer program to put together a whole lot of pictures, and even some film (so he said). I didn't tell him, but I was actually looking forward to when we would all present our assignments. He'd chosen an awesome topic.

Dad came in at one stage and asked whether we had other homework to do. 'Yeah, sure, Dad,' I replied. 'I'll get on with it after the others leave.'

As Dad was rummaging through some of my books, a little card fell out. I hadn't even noticed it myself.

'Hey, this sounds good,' he said. 'You never told me about the MCG excursion. How was it?'

'Bit weird,' Jay said before I had a chance to speak.

'Nah, it was okay, Dad. There was this nice old guy ...'

'Strange, more like it.'

I glared at Jay.

'This nice old guy who was looking after the library there. He must have slipped that card into one of my books when they were on the table.'

'Well,' said Dad, 'it sounds interesting enough. "Slip through the ages of time. A journey of discovery for all your cricket research. Get lost in another world." Well, well. Rather a full-on advertisement for a library of old books, eh, boys?'

Dad loved his cricket as much as anyone.

'Let's all go down sometime soon, hey? I'd love to see this place. Maybe Georgie would like to come, as well? You could all do some more work on your projects.'

Dad liked Georgie. Being a bit of a writer himself, he was forever talking poems and stuff with her when she came round. And Georgie, of course, loved the attention.

'Yeah, that would be great, Dad,' I said as he flipped the card over to me.

'Sounds good to me, Mr Jones,' added Rahul.

'Great. How about Wednesday? Cricket training's on Tuesday and Thursday, isn't it?'

'Wednesday'd be great, Dad,' I said, not sure if I was ready to go back to the library just yet.

BATTING – WORKING TOGETHER

Batting is a partnership. It's 11 against two. And two is a whole lot better than one. Take the opportunity at the end of overs to talk to your partner. Offer advice and encouragement. Tell your partner how well he or she is playing. Sometimes it can be too easy for the fielding team to gain a psychological edge over the batters because they outnumber them, or they get vocally enthusiastic! Always remember: it's 11 against two.

It's your job to try to rebalance the situation by coming across as strong and confident. Appear in control of the situation, even if you don't feel in control.

A few good overs, a couple of fours, can make a huge difference in your outlook. As a batting partnership, you should set yourselves goals.

You might want to work at pushing some quick singles, or perhaps bat in 15 minute blocks.

Above all, support and encourage your partner. With any luck, you will be supported and encouraged in turn.

Between March 1979 and March 1994 Allan Border (Australia) did not miss a Test match. This amounted to 153 consecutive Test match appearances. This put Border 47 Test matches ahead of his nearest rival, Sunil Gavaskar, from India.

4 The Gym

Tuesday — afternoon

THE gym was booked, Georgie hadn't forgotten. I often met up with others there at the start of lunchtime and usually other kids would call by and end up joining in. Even Jimbo had stopped in for a look one lunchtime a few weeks back. He sat on one of the long benches at the back of the gym and watched. He was eating a salad roll. I remember this because you are not allowed to eat in the gym. But no one was going to mention this little rule to Jimbo.

We played with three pieces of equipment: a stump for a bat, a set of kanga wickets and a tennis ball that was half-covered with black tape. It swung like crazy.

We picked a couple of teams.

'Where's your secret friend?' I asked Georgie as I took my place behind the stumps to be keeper. Martian, the regular keeper, said he had a bit of a headache and was sitting out this game.

'She'll be here soon. And when she gets here, I want her to have a go at keeper, okay?'

'Yeah, sure,' I said.

Rahul whacked the first ball back past Jay and into the back wall for four. He had a great eye — even if he did wear glasses — and it always looked as if he was playing with a real bat.

'Hey Georgie, I'm here.'

A tall girl with long hair was standing at the door. I had seen her before, though she wasn't in any of my classes.

'Hey, Ally,' Georgie called out. 'Get in here. Toby, get out in the field, would you? Ally, go behind the stumps and just grab the ball if it comes your way, okay?'

'Watch out, Marshall, looks like a girl's gonna take your keeping job,' said Scott Craven, who had just arrived with Gavin Bourke. I wondered if they had come with Ally.

I looked over at Martian to see if he would react to this teasing from Craven. But amazingly, he had his eyes closed and his head tilted up towards the roof.

I walked over to him.

'Hey, Martian, you okay?'

He didn't open his eyes, but smiled slightly and put one thumb up in the air. 'Sort of. Bit of a headache, but I'll be okay.'

Meanwhile, Ally had got herself behind the stumps, and was waiting for Jay to bowl. It was a wide one. Ally took it easily and flicked it back, low and hard, to Jay.

'Okay? Now can I go?'

'Ally! C'mon,' said Georgie. 'You said you'd stay for at least 10 minutes.'

'Okay, 10 minutes. Nine now. Let's do it!'

She was amazing. She didn't miss a ball. And most of the deliveries went to her as most of us still couldn't hit the ball with a stump. Her throws were neat and strong, too. True to her word, though, she waved goodbye to Georgie about 10 minutes later and headed out the door.

'Hey, Ally, did you enjoy it?' Georgie called.

'Yeah. Actually it was good. I'd like to stay, but I've got some stuff to catch up on.'

'Ally's a good keeper, huh?' Georgie said, as we headed off to afternoon class.

'Awesome,' I replied.

'She plays representative softball. She's the catcher. I just thought it would be interesting to see if she could handle being a keeper.'

'No problems there. Does she want to play?' I asked.

'Not sure.'

'You want to add to that answer?' Jay asked.

Georgie thought for a moment.

'No.'

'Pity,' Jay responded.

We all turned. Martian had joined us, obviously having heard our conversation. Suddenly he stopped and headed for the library.

'Hey, Martian,' Georgie called out, 'I don't mean for her to take your place.'

But Martian didn't turn around. He kept on walking.

'Bummer! Toby, will you see him in class this arvo?' Georgie asked.

'Yeah, I'll talk to him.'

'Thanks. I really didn't mean it like that. It's just that it'd be nice to have another girl in the team, you know.'

'Yeah, I know,' I said.

As it turned out, I didn't catch up with Martian during the afternoon. He didn't show up at all. Instead, I spent a lot of the lesson thinking about how weird the MCG excursion had been. Jay didn't seem to want anything to do with it and Georgie didn't believe me. At least she didn't believe the time travel bit. I needed to talk to someone smart, someone straight. Someone who'd call it as he saw it. I thought of Jimbo.

Jimbo always took a bus home from school, but it didn't leave until 10 to four. I seized my moment.

'Hiya, Jimbo.'

He looked at me and nodded. Not mean, or angry. Almost a bit surprised.

'Can I ask you something?'

Again Jimbo nodded, without speaking.

'Well, you know how we had that excursion last week, and I went to the MCG? Well, there was

34

this guy, an old guy ... like, a really old guy actually ...'

'Yeah?'

'His name's Jim. Jim Oldfield.'

Jimbo was looking at me politely, waiting for me to finish.

'Well, he told me some really weird stuff —'

'Like what?'

It was hard to know where to start, as I knew the whole thing was going to sound stupid. A bus pulled up. Jimbo turned to look at it, then turned back to me.

'So?'

'Nah, it's okay, Jimbo. Doesn't matter. Is that your bus?'

'Nope. Tell me, Toby. What did he say? You said it was weird. I want to know.'

It took a few minutes, but I told him everything. I even dragged the poem out of my pocket and showed it to him. Jimbo didn't say anything. He just shook his head and whistled softly.

Another bus had pulled up.

'This one's mine. See ya, and thanks for telling me all that.'

He picked up his bag and climbed onto the bus.

And then I realised that I hadn't asked him the one question I really wanted to know the answer to: why he wouldn't, or couldn't, play cricket for us. Maybe one day I would go and visit Jimbo and try to find out.

PRACTICE — MAKING IT TOUGH

There are many examples of famous cricketers making practice conditions especially hard for themselves so they could improve their skills. Rodney Marsh, the great Australian wicket keeper of the 1970s and early 1980s, used to throw a golf ball at the pole of a clothesline. He worked on improving his reflexes by catching the ball as it came off at all sorts of angles. And there is, of course, the famous film of Donald Bradman tossing a golf ball against the side of a corrugated iron water tank, then hitting the ball with a stump.

It's a good idea to try to hit a ball using a stump, or even a section of broom handle, for a bat. The next time you play with a real bat, it will feel a lot wider than it really is, giving your confidence a boost and perhaps turning a small score into a big one.

In an 1884 Test match between Australia and England, all 11 players, including the keeper, got to bowl for England. Guess who got the most wickets? Yes! The keeper! His figures were 12 overs, 5 maidens, 4/19. The first 200 scored in a Test match occurred in this game: Billy Murdoch made 211 out of Australia's 551.

5 The Cricketer

Wednesday — afternoon

WHEN school finished I walked over to the car park behind the gym and met up with Jay and Rahul. Georgie arrived a few minutes later. She was coming to the MCG too and then staying at my house for dinner.

'Did you speak to Martian, Toby?' Georgie asked.

'I didn't see him all day. He told me in the gym at lunchtime yesterday that he was feeling sick, so maybe he went home.'

'Georgie, get real. Your friend Ally won't play cricket. She's too pretty to play cricket.'

Oh, boy. Jay had just put his foot in it. Big time.

'What?' Georgie said to him, in a hissing tone.

'Well, I mean, she doesn't look the type, that's all,' Jay stammered.

'Georgie, tell Ally what Jay said and then maybe she'll play cricket,' said Rahul.

We all looked at him, a bit perplexed.

'You lot coming to the MCG?' a voice yelled at us from an open car window a moment later.

Dad had arrived.

We piled our bags into the boot and jumped in.

'Crikey, you kids don't know how lucky you are. Getting to do projects on cricket! Can you believe it? In my day it was the Battle of Hastings and the Peasants' Revolt.'

Dad chatted most of the way, and each of us was left to our own thoughts. I could imagine what some of those thoughts were.

Georgie would be wondering about how to get Ally playing cricket without hurting Martian's feelings. Jay would be angry with himself for saying the first thing that came into his head, and he'd be thinking of a way to get back into Georgie's good books.

'Hey Georgie, you want me to try to hunt out that book of cricket poems my uncle gave me for Christmas last year?'

(See, what did I tell you?)

And Rahul? Actually, I wouldn't have a clue what Rahul would be thinking. I turned to look at him. He was staring out the window and smiling as we turned into the MCG car park. Probably smiling at Jay's comment. Then again, it's just as likely that he was thinking about something else.

As for me, I was getting a bit nervous about seeing Jim again, especially having Dad and the others with me.

* * *

But as it happened, I was in for a big disappointment. Or maybe it was relief. After we'd shown the little card to the lady at the desk, we were taken up to the old part of the stand. On the walls of the passageways were the old photographs and massive paintings. Cricket bats stood in a glass cabinet. Some of the old ones looked like paddles for a little rowing boat. When we walked into the library, there was no one sitting at the oval table. There was no pile of books lying scattered across it. The glass doors of the bookshelves were shut. They looked as if they hadn't been opened in years.

The only person in the room was a man sitting in a green chair over to the left of the room. His glasses were pushed up on his forehead and a closed book lay in his lap. He appeared to be asleep.

Jay looked at me and smiled.

'Just as well he's not here, I reckon. Let's forget it ever happened, eh?'

For a moment I was about to agree. But then I noticed the rows of brown and yellow *Wisden Almanacks* lined up across the top shelves. I walked over to them, reached up and tried to open the cabinet door. It was locked.

'Found something interesting, mate?' Dad asked me.

'*Wisdens*, Dad. There's one for every year since way back, with all the scores and stuff from every game played in that year.' Dad was nodding his head and sighing.

'Well not quite every game, my boy, but all the important ones.'

My heart stopped. I wheeled around and found myself staring at a smiling Jim. I smiled too. The secret door in the wall had opened and closed. Dad was looking confused, though I felt safe with him standing next to me.

Dad held out his hand and introduced himself.

'Good to meet you, Peter,' Jim said, nodding his head as Dad introduced the others to him.

'The kids are all doing cricket projects at school. They probably told you.' Dad was prattling on. 'That was a very kind invitation of yours, Jim. And what a treasury of old books.'

'And some not so old, either, Peter.'

Dad was nodding enthusiastically.

'Right then, everyone. What are you all studying again?' asked Dad. There was something tense and unsure about the moment, and I think Dad was picking up the vibes.

'Well I'm doing women in cricket. 'I'm really interested in what I've read about women inventing over-arm bowling.'

Georgie had spoken up, of course, and Jim moved over to a small table, grabbed a set of keys from a drawer and limped off to a distant bookcase.

'Excellent, excellent!' Dad was excited. He led us over to the table and we took out our folders to get stuck into a bit of serious research. It looked as if time travel was off the agenda — for that day, at least.

When everyone had settled down to a bit of study,

I sneaked a look at Jim. He was smiling at me. It was a gentle smile.

'Peter, did you ever play cricket?' Jim was still looking at me.

Dad looked up from where he was sitting on the floor with a huge book open on his knees.

'Yes, I played a bit.'

Dad had never spoken much about his cricket-playing days. Well, to me he had, but the others didn't really know that he used to play at a pretty high level. 'At school,' he added.

'And what about after school?' said Jim.

Dad looked at me. He shrugged.

'Yes, and after school.'

'Where, Mr Jones?' Rahul asked. 'Who for?'

'You don't want to hear . . .'

'Toby's dad here played for Victoria,' Jim chimed in, his eyebrows raised.

I sensed the others looking up from their books.

'They don't want to know about that,' said Dad, staring at Jim.

There was an uneasy silence.

'Wow, Mr Jones, that is so cool! Did you play here, at the "G"?' Georgie asked

Dad closed the book he was holding and said, 'Well, Jim, I fear a little cat has been let out of a bag. You say those brown and yellow books up there have all the games played? Well, let's pull down a few from the '80s and see if we can find a Jones among a few others more famous.'

'No!' I jumped up from my seat.

'It's all right, Toby,' said Jim.

Dad was looking at me strangely.

Jim had pulled down a *Wisden*. It had a hard yellow cover. I didn't see the year. The others had gathered around. Jim was flicking through the pages. I couldn't bear to look.

'Here we are. Victoria versus South Australia. At the MCG.'

Slowly I looked up from the table in front of me to the open pages of the book. The letters and numbers swirled and blended, spinning round and round in a sea of black and white. I closed my eyes.

'Here, let's have a look,' Dad said, reaching out for the book.

'No!' I yelled again.

But before I had a chance to stop him, Jim had passed the book over to Dad. I looked at Dad's face. He was smiling.

'It's all right, Toby. They don't bite. I think I've got a few of them stashed away somewhere. Ah, here we are! P. Jones, bowled, for 23. That was my highest score for Victoria. Jim, you've found the best page about me!'

'Dad, you can read it?'

'Yeeeees,' he said slowly, 'I picked up that handy skill about 35 years ago. Hadn't I told you that?'

'Did you get a bowl, Mr Jones? Or take a catch?' Rahul asked.

'Nope. Nothing. We won the game, though.'

Dad closed the book and handed it back to Jim.

'Do you know, I can remember that game quite well,' Jim said, nodding thoughtfully. 'I was here in the library and I had a visitor. Quite a young visitor. Though unfortunately we never met. A most curious thing it was.' It sounded as if Jim was rambling.

'Well, I think we've probably taken up enough of your time, Jim.'

'Oh, yes, by all means, yes indeed,' Jim replied, though a bit hazily.

As Dad helped the others put their books away, Jim quietly called my name, then spoke softly.

'Have you ever heard of talents skipping a generation? They say it of music and musicians. When my father read *Wisdens*, he read *Wisdens*. When I read *Wisdens*, I travel through time. Just as my grandfather did. I think it's the same with you, Toby. Of course I can read the words now, too. That takes time to learn, as you will discover.'

'Okay then, people, ready to go?' called Dad.

'Can you all come again? It's wonderful to see young people here learning about cricket.'

'I'm sure they'd love to. What do you think, kids?'

Rahul and Georgie nodded. Jay was looking down at his shoes. I mumbled something that meant nothing.

'Well, I think I can persuade them, Jim. As long as you don't reveal any more secrets about me.'

They both laughed as we headed out.

On 15 March 1877 a player gained a record that may never be broken. He represented England in the first official Test match played against Australia. He holds the record for being the oldest player to ever represent his or her country on debut. His name was J. Southerton – he was an off-spin bowler and he was 49 years and 119 days old.

6 The Past

Wednesday — evening

WE dropped off Rahul and Jay. Georgie had picked up on my weird behaviour — unlike Dad, who was sometimes a bit vague about things around him.

This time Georgie's approach was different. She got all efficient. She knew me as well as anyone, and sensed that something had been going on in the MCC library that afternoon.

We headed for the computer. Georgie opened up a new document and started to type up a summary of all the important facts.

1. *Old Jim works in the library at the MCG*   *(fact)*
2. *There are heaps of* Wisdens *in the library*   *(fact)*
3. *When Toby looks at a* Wisden, *the words go swirly (?)*
4. *Jim says you can travel back in time*   *(???)*
5. *No one else seems to see the swirly writing*   *(fact)*

We figured the only solution was for us to head down to the MCG on Friday after school and, once and for all, get to the bottom of the whole thing with Jim.

'And what? We just walk through the gate and straight up to the library?' Georgie asked.

I pulled out the little card that Dad had read aloud on Monday.

'I think taking this means that you're allowed to go up and do cricket research,' I said.

'Okay, bring it. And bring the poem too,' she added.

Thursday — morning

At recess I headed for the gym hoping to catch Jimbo there. I still wanted to ask him why he hadn't played in the game on Saturday.

Once again he looked at me without saying anything. For a moment I thought he wouldn't reply. Finally he said, 'Too busy.'

'Geez, it's a pity. You're such a good bat.'

'Thanks, Toby. You're a great bowler. No, my dad's trying to teach me that there's more to life than just cricket. I do other things on a Saturday.'

'More to life than cricket?' I shook my head.

Jimbo smiled. 'We have weekend projects. At the moment we're clearing out the garage.' I must have been looking a bit sorry for Jimbo. Not being able to play cricket on a Saturday sounded pretty disastrous to me. Cleaning out a garage just made it worse.

'It's okay, Toby. One day I'll play in real games.'

'Well I hope we're on the same side when you do.'

'Yeah, me too.'

'You want to come over to the nets with the others then?' I asked him.

46

Jimbo looked at his watch.

'The bell's going pretty soon. Another time, maybe?'

I was halfway over to the nets when the bell did go. I turned back to look at Jimbo.

'See you at training,' he called.

Thursday — afternoon

We were in the nets. Mr Pasquali took one of the nets himself and threw ball after ball at a couple of batters who he said were sluggish with their feet. Mr Pasquali was a great coach. He took the time to talk to you about your batting and bowling. And fielding too. As I padded up for my turn, I watched him working on Jono's front foot, on-side attacking shots. He made you feel like a real cricketer.

We hung around after practice, waiting for the team to get put up on the notice board, but Mr Pasquali, who had been on the phone, came out of the gym and said we'd have to wait till tomorrow. He looked worried.

Martian wasn't at training, and I wondered if that had anything to do with Mr Pasquali's behaviour. Whatever it was, it didn't look like good news.

That night I lay in bed for a long time thinking about Jimbo cleaning out the garage, about Mr Pasquali looking worried, and about Jim in the library. Perhaps this was my chance to see some other cricket matches. Maybe some famous ones. Maybe the World Cup. My mind drifted to stories that Dad told me about amazing cricket games. Like the time he lay on his mum's and dad's bed listening to the radio, not daring to move as Allan Border and Jeff Thomson got closer and closer to achieving an incredible victory. It was in the early '80s. Dad said that he lay totally still on the bed. He thought that if he moved, the spell would be broken and one of the batters would be dismissed, leaving England as the winners.

They were the last pair. I can remember the scores easily. Thomson came in on the fourth day, when the score was 218. Australia needed 292 to win — 74 runs. England only needed 1 wicket. And they had a whole day and a bit to get it. But by the end of that day Australia had knocked off 37 of the runs. Which was exactly half the runs they needed to make.

The next morning, according to Dad, radios were on everywhere. Cars had pulled over. Maybe the drivers were getting stressed out with the tension. People were hanging around in shops listening to the game. Dad said that they let people in for free on that final morning. They were expecting a couple of thousand people. Eighteen thousand turned out to watch the game. I reckon I would have, too.

Border and Thomson (he was a fast bowler and the number 11 batsman) batted on and on. They refused to take singles. They got to 288 — only 4 runs from victory — when Thomson edged a ball into the slips. The first guy got his hands to it, and managed to bump it up so that the second slip fielder caught the ball just before it hit the ground.

Dad said he cried.

And then there was Hobart. The Test match against Pakistan when Adam Gilchrist and Justin Langer put on an amazing partnership to first rescue Australia, who were 5 for 126 in their second innings, and then take them on to victory. They had a partnership of over 340 runs!

Dad also talked about a fast bowler from New Zealand called Richard Hadlee. He's a knight now. I sure would like to see him bowl. Dad said that in one Test match he totally cleaned up Australia, taking 8 wickets in an innings.

Actually, Dad's a bit like Mr Pasquali. He's a guy who loves his cricket. I wonder if Dad's all-time dream was to play for his country. This got me wondering about all the cricketers who had played for Australia. Did Don Bradman have the dream? What about all the players now? Did they lie in bed at night staring at their bedroom walls thinking of 60,000 people roaring and cheering as they walked out to play?

My last thought before falling asleep was that there was no way I was going to miss out on what Jim and the *Wisden* books were possibly offering. Didn't Jim say that this was a once in a lifetime opportunity?

Friday — afternoon

Georgie and I had no trouble getting permission to visit the library at the MCG. We caught the tram and were going to be picked up later. I was beginning to feel at home there. This was only my third visit, but the quiet and the calm in the little library gave it an almost magical feel. It almost seemed wrong to speak in there.

The man with glasses was there again, this time reading a book. He looked up as we entered, smiled briefly, then went back to his reading.

A moment later Jim appeared, hobbling slowly towards us from behind a table.

'Hello, Toby, Georgie.'

'Hello, Jim.'

I thought back to last night. To the cricket matches I'd recalled Dad talking about. And to the many more I'd dreamed about.

'I'm ready,' I told him, firmly.

'Yes, I know you are.' Jim walked over to the glass cabinet and pulled down a *Wisden* from the shelf. It was the 2000 edition.

'The 1999 World Cup, Toby. That's what you're studying, isn't it?'

I nodded, keeping my eyes on the book Jim was thumbing through.

Georgie hadn't said a word, which was surprising for her. But now she was reaching into her pocket, and yanking out a creased copy of the poem I had emailed to her.

'Great poem, Mr Oldfield,' she said to him.

Jim paused from his browsing and looked at Georgie.

'My father wrote that many years ago. Actually, they are the words of my grandfather.'

'Yes, well I was just wondering about the word "dead".'

Jim winced.

'Whose lives are dead?' she asked.

'I wonder, my dear, would you mind hopping along to the kitchen and getting me a glass of water? It's just down the hall to your right.'

Georgie and I stared at him.

'Excuse me?' Georgie said.

'I just wondered ...'

With a sigh, Georgie walked to the door.

'Toby,' said Jim firmly when she had gone. 'It's now or never. Come on.'

Jim passed Georgie's copy of the poem to me. He gestured for me to follow him. We moved to a place behind the shelves, slightly around the corner from the main part of the library, and hidden from the front section where the big oval table stood.

The man in the chair hadn't moved.

'Toby, look at me. If this should work, and you find yourself in a strange place, read aloud two lines from the poem. Straight away. Do you understand? Straight away. You only ever have two hours, anyway — the time it takes to complete a session of cricket. Toby, how long?'

'Two hours,' I breathed, startled at Jim's urgency and energy. He nodded.

'Now, I want you to focus hard on the page here and try to stop the words and numbers moving.'

He passed the book across to me. Everything was happening in a rush. Georgie would be back in a

51

moment, but for some reason I didn't want her to return. Not yet, anyway. I looked down at the open book that Jim was holding. The swirl of black and white was no different from last time.

'The top of the page, Toby. Concentrate. Try to make the words settle. Force the letters to stop moving. Then say the word that appears.'

I shook my head and lifted my eyes to the top of the page. There was less black here, but still the swirly effect continued. I wasn't sure what I was supposed to be doing, but as I thought of asking Jim, I sensed the page settling. I hadn't looked at a *Wisden* page yet for as long as this. For a moment, I thought I could make out a word. Then it went washy again.

'Keep at it, Toby. Keep going,' Jim urged.

Another word drifted in, then away, but this time I could read the word. 'South.' I didn't dare look down the page, where I still sensed a flurry of black marks swishing and surging like ants in cream.

'What can you see, Toby? Can you read to me?'

'S-S-South Africa,' I stammered, peering into the mess. 'Oh, hang on. It's a date, June, I think, and there's a ...'

Someone was speaking.

Something about a glass of water ...

I looked up. A roar surrounded me. I stood, transfixed.

Utterly confused.

I thumped myself, to feel my own body, and swung around. I was surrounded by people, but no one was paying me the slightest attention. There was no carpet beneath me. Just grey concrete.

The bright light was glaring. There was a gasp from the crowd and then applause. I couldn't help myself. I looked out towards the players. Someone had just belted a four.

I took another glance around me. There was a lot of noise and chatter. I noticed some empty seats about 10 metres away. Nervously I walked to them and sat down. I felt as if everyone should be looking at me, but when I turned to check, people were just concentrating on the cricket.

I checked the scoreboard. Australia were batting. South Africa were in the field. I was in England, in the year 1999, watching the World Cup semi-final! Steve Waugh and Michael Bevan were in. The score was 4 for 86. Bevan was on 6 and Steve Waugh was on 13. I suddenly realised that no one here knew what was going to happen. They didn't know that they were going to see one of the most exciting finishes to a cricket game ever — well, that's what Dad and I thought.

I opened my mouth to speak, then quickly closed it again. Maybe now wasn't the right time to be showing off my knowledge.

I looked around at the people beside me.

'They're struggling, aren't they?' A lady was speaking to me from two seats away. She was the first person who appeared to have noticed me.

I opened my mouth but nothing came out.

'You alright then, love?' she asked. She had an English accent.

I nodded.

'Where are you from then?'

'Australia.' The word came out a bit garbled, but she'd heard me.

'Oooh, really? Well, you'd better hope that Bevan and Waugh put on a partnership, otherwise you're done for.'

Someone started talking to her and she turned away. I turned back to the cricket. I felt calmer when I was watching it. I took a few deep breaths then closed and opened my eyes a few times. Nothing changed.

A surge of excitement and exhilaration charged through me. Jim was right. I had travelled in time. I really was here at the World Cup! It was the most awesome and spectacular thing imaginable.

But then a thought occurred to me. How long had I been away? Was the time I was spending here the same as the time that Jim and Georgie were spending at the library?

I decided to give it one more over. That couldn't hurt. Allan Donald was bowling and Bevan was facing. He didn't look in any hurry to score. But that was okay. He actually let the third ball go through to the keeper, but he scored a run off the second-last ball and then Steve Waugh scored a single off the last.

'Not your seat, I don't think, lad.'

I turned around. A couple of men were standing over me. The first guy was holding three plastic cups.

I stood up and scuttled past them and back to the spot where I'd arrived. I took out the scrap of paper with the poem on it and read out the first two lines I saw:

> *Now, hide your home, your age, your soul*
> *To roam this place and seek your goal.*

'What?' someone was saying loudly, close by me.

'Georgie?' I gasped.

'What are you doing?' She looked at me queerly. 'You look as if you've seen a ghost.' I looked down, this time at red and blue carpet.

'Where's Jim?' I whispered.

'Over there, sipping his water.'

In a daze, I walked past Georgie and over to Jim. He looked up from his book, his eyes shining.

I stared at him. I swallowed. I was totally speechless.

'What?'

Georgie had followed me and was looking at both of us in turn.

'You said you liked the poem, young lady?' said Jim, still looking at me. He had a habit of doing that.

'Yes,' she replied. 'So?'

'I think Toby here thinks it's quite a special poem too, eh, Toby?'

'Yes.' It came as a croak. 'Yes,' I repeated. 'How long was I there, Jim?'

'What? Where?' Georgie was getting exasperated.

'Or would you like to know how long you were away?' Jim was smiling. 'How long did it feel like?' he asked.

'About five minutes,' I replied, 'but it must have been longer.'

'Remember the words of the poem, Toby.

Your time, this time; none short, or long

'The time matches up quite closely, you know, though it can distort if you travel quite a way back,' Jim said. 'But don't forget, two hours is your limit.'

I had a hundred questions to ask Jim. I was still in shock, and I suppose if I'd stopped a moment and thought about what had just happened I would have run out of the room, never to return. Ever! But I didn't move.

Even though I'd told Georgie about the time travelling she didn't seem to realise where I'd been, although she knew that something weird had happened. I grabbed her hand and the 2000 *Wisden* that was lying on the table in front of Jim.

'Toby, not yet!'

Jim had risen, his hands stretched out towards me, for the book. I looked at him. His face seemed concerned.

'Please, Toby, don't be foolish. You're not ready to carry. To take others with you,' he added when he saw my questioning look.

Georgie flung my hand out of hers and jolted me round.

'What are you doing, Toby?' she yelled.

'Georgie, you'll never believe me otherwise. Never. I've got to take you there. Please?'

'Take me where, you idiot? Behind the shelves for a quick kiss? Is that what you mean?'

I couldn't believe what she was saying.

Slowly I walked back to the table and sat down. I placed the *Wisden Almanack* down in front of Jim, who was sitting down again too. He pushed his half-empty glass of water across the table to me. I reached out, took a gulp and sighed.

'Okay. Good. All is calm, all is bright. All is splendid on Friday night.'

'Thanks for that, Georgie,' I said to her.

'My pleasure. What now?'

'Georgie, you're a breath of fresh air,' said Jim with a smile.

'Probably more like hot air, Mr Oldfield,' she replied, almost breaking into a smile herself.

'Well, enough adventures for one afternoon, don't you think?' Jim said.

'Yeah, I guess. Getting that water was just non-stop action and excitement for me. I couldn't go through that again.'

At least Georgie had recovered her sense of humour.

PRACTICE — IN THE NETS

Net sessions can be very helpful, if done correctly. A batter has the opportunity to focus on a particular area of his or her batting. Being surrounded by netting means that there is little time wasted in retrieving balls — either hit or missed. A batter can face many deliveries in a short space of time.

If a particular stroke needs to be practised, balls can be thrown to give the batter the chance to play the stroke again and again. This should develop his or her skill and technique, as well as confidence.

It is important for bowlers to concentrate on their work, too. Make sure that you have at least one stump to run past at the bowler's end and that you're using a reasonable cricket ball. Bowling with an old, tattered, or soft ball may not inspire you to work hard enough. And be sure not to bowl no-balls. Your run-up is as important in the nets as in a match.

Finally, keep alert. Never turn your back to the batters. You may cop a full-blooded drive from the next net!

The lowest number of runs scored in a day of Test cricket was 95. This happened in Karachi, Pakistan on 11 October 1956. On that day Australia were dismissed for 80, and Pakistan, at stumps, were 2/15 in reply. This was also the only day of cricket ever attended by a President of the USA, Dwight Eisenhower!

7 The Run-out

Saturday — morning

IT was a classic summer's day. By 8.30 the temperature had already gone past 25°C. Today was our first two-day game, but I was glad the games would be over by lunchtime.

I wolfed down some toast and checked my cricket kit for the seventh time that morning. Mum headed out early — she was taking Nat to her tennis game.

'Good luck, Toby. Hope all goes well,' she called from the door.

'Thanks, Mum. Hey, good luck to you too, Nat!' I called.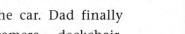

I was ready and sitting in the car. Dad finally arrived with all his gear: camera, deckchair, binoculars, mobile phone, wallet and sunglasses. After a stop at the local milk bar he'd have even more stuff — newspapers and some drinks and snacks. It was Dad's favourite time of the week, I'm sure of it.

* * *

Jono won the toss and we batted. We would bat for three and a half hours, and then the following Saturday, St Mary's, the team we were playing, would bat for the same number of overs as they bowled to us today. I'd checked out their form in the paper. They had lost to TCC by about 20 runs, and TCC weren't supposed to be very strong either.

It was a good day not to be standing out in the field. And it was good to empty my brain of time travel, Jim, poems, kissing Georgie and all that had been happening this week. I loved playing cricket. I loved getting involved in the game I was playing. It was like going to the movies. You lost your sense of anything that was going on elsewhere, and what time it was.

Again there was no Jimbo, and no Martian either. Mr Pasquali told us that Martian had been involved in a car accident and would be missing a bit of school. Rahul would have been wicket keeper if we'd been bowling.

'Maybe Martian will be right to keep next week, Mr Pasquali?' asked Cameron, putting on his pads. He was our other opener, a neat, left-handed batter with a rock-solid defence.

'Yes, Cam, maybe.'

Mr Pasquali didn't sound very hopeful. But he looked as if he didn't want to say any more. Maybe that was the phone call he got at training last Thursday.

'Is he okay?' Georgie asked.

The whole team had gone quiet. Mr Pasquali looked around at us.

'Ivo's going to be fine, everyone. He's been quite shaken up and is going to need some time in hospital to recover.' Mr Pasquali nodded. The matter was over.

'Okay, plenty of time, people,' Mr Pasquali said. 'Let's knock up a few 40s today. It's a fast outfield and we've got some short boundaries square of the wicket. Respect the good balls, and belt the wide ones, but keep them along the ground.'

'Unless you reckon you can go over the top,' added Scott Craven, staring out at the witches' hats and licking his lips with anticipation.

'Each ball on its merit, Scott,' Mr Pasquali said, shaking his head.

Scott Craven could tear a bowling attack apart with his tremendous hitting. I'd picked his bat up once, a few weeks back, at practice. He'd seen me almost straight away. For a moment I thought he was going to belt me with it. But instead, he'd strolled over, smiling.

'It weighs a tonne!' I'd told him.

'It's a 16-kilo slugging machine,' he'd said, taking it from me and twisting it in the air. Then he'd aimed a cut shot at my head.

'And it would knock your head off, Tobias.'

He had a nasty habit of using my full name. No one else ever did.

I'd nodded slowly. 'Guess it would, Scott.'

I'd mumbled a few more not-so-choice words under my breath as I headed out to the nets.

St Mary's had an accurate attack and we were scoring at about 3 an over. Georgie was doing her usual routine. She was already padded up, even though she wasn't due to go in until 5 wickets had fallen. I had the pads on too, but I was batting fourth. One in front of Scott.

By the time I walked out to bat, the sun was beating down and the bowlers were looking tired. They'd been out there for an hour and a half, and had only taken 1 wicket: Cameron caught at mid-off for 27. We were 1 for 95. Scott Craven came in after Rahul retired on 42. The first ball he faced he padded back down the wicket. The second, he smashed way over mid-wicket for six.

He strolled down at the end of the over and told me to feed him the strike because he was feeling 'like a good hit-out'. But disaster struck soon after. Scott was getting impatient watching me block the first few balls I faced. Mr Pasquali had said we had plenty of time, and I was just getting my eye in, but Scott was becoming annoyed.

'C'mon, Toby, look for the gaps,' he called out to me.

Finally, I nudged the last ball of the over out between cover and point. There was an easy single. I called Scott through. He wasn't moving.

'Yes!' I shouted. I couldn't believe he wasn't

running. By now I was halfway up the pitch. The fielder had run back to where the ball had stopped and was picking it up. I don't know why, especially as it was Scott standing at the other end, but I kept on running. Scott had moved a few metres out of his crease, not aware that I had now passed him and made it across the line.

The ball was tossed to the keeper, who gently knocked one bail off the stumps.

'You idiot, Jones. You've just gone and run yourself out!'

But the umpire had different ideas. 'You're out, son,' he said, looking at Scott.

Then I did a really weak thing. I knew who was out too. Perhaps I was after a bit of respect from Scott.

'It's okay, I'll go,' I said to the umpire.

'No, you actually crossed, so you're not out. This feller is.'

Scott was going white with anger. Not red. The umpire obviously didn't know him. 'Off you go, son,' he said cheerfully, then raised his finger to confirm, publicly, that a run-out had just occurred. Amid the cheers of the fielders now running in towards the pitch, Scott glared at me, then shook his head. I knew I was going to hear more about this.

Gavin Bourke, Scott's best mate, strode out to the wicket. I saw Scott hurl his bat onto the grass, then throw down his gloves. He turned around again and glared across the oval at me.

'You're in deep, mate,' Gavin said cheerfully. 'Which end am I at?'

I pointed down to the other end where the umpire had moved into position for the next over. My mouth was dry.

Both Jono and Rahul came back and made their 50s. This probably made Scott even madder. If he'd batted through to his 40, he would have got another bat too. I reckon there could have been 100 out there for him today, given the tired bowling and the short boundaries. We made 271.

'Don't forget, it wasn't your fault,' Georgie told me at the end of the innings. 'Scott's just so greedy that he didn't want you to take a single off the last ball of the over.'

'It was my call. I called, and he didn't respond.'

'Yep,' she agreed. 'There was an easy single there. It looked as if you were about to walk yourself.'

'I was.' I wasn't looking at Georgie. 'I just thought it'd be easier if I went. You know how he gets.'

'Toby, he gets his way so often. He doesn't need favours from you as well.'

'You're right.'

'Toby?'

'Yeah.'

'You don't need his respect, either. C'mon. I've got some jobs to do for Mum, then she said I could come round to your place and watch the cricket on TV. What do you say?'

'Brilliant.'

We packed up our gear and headed over to Dad's car.

BATTING — MAKING THE RIGHT CALL

To avoid being run out there are some important rules to remember when you're batting. There are three calls that batters should make when deciding to run or not: Yes, No or Wait. Saying 'Go!' is definitely to be avoided. It sounds too much like 'No!'. Generally, if the ball is played in front of the batter, then that person — the striker — should make the call. If the ball goes behind the batter, the non-striker should make the call. Sometimes you can't do anything about a freakish piece of fielding. You just have to run like crazy, reach forward with your bat as you near the crease and hope that the stumps haven't been broken by the time your bat crosses that line.

In 1890, in a game in Victoria between Portland and Port Fairy, a square-leg umpire, Umpire Threlfall, fielded the ball then hurled it back, hitting the stumps, before he realised that he wasn't actually a fielder. Amid howls of laughter, one of the fielders appealed.

The umpire had to say, 'Not out!'

8 The Mistake

Monday — morning

FOR a couple of classes that morning, we went to the library to work on our cricket projects. I was sitting next to Rahul, who was struggling with his Madras Test match. He had plenty of books on India but not much on the actual game itself.

'Hey Rahul, why don't you interview one of the players from the game?' I suggested.

He looked at me and smiled.

'Right, so I just go and ring up Dean Jones or Greg Matthews or Allan Border and ask them if I can interview them?' he joked.

'Well, yeah. Who else played in the game?' I asked. 'Any other Victorians?'

'There was Ray Bright. He took seven wickets in the game. Five in the second innings,' Rahul answered.

'It can't be too hard. We could ask Mr Pasquali. Or look up, say, Dean Jones on the Internet or in the telephone book. We could find him. Do it!'

'Do what?'

'Ring him! Go visit! Do an interview. It'd be awesome!'

'Oh, right. I just go and look up Dean Jones in the phone book and tell him I want an interview. How many Joneses are there in the phone book? You reckon his name will have "Test cricketer" beside it? And even if I do get to speak to him, do you think he'd waste his time talking to a kid? Like he's got nothing better to do.'

'Well, you might need to get Mr Pasquali or your dad to make the first call. You know, set it up for you,' I said.

Rahul thought for a moment. 'I guess it's worth a try. It'd be brilliant if it came off. I suppose it'd be almost as good as being at the game. Okay Toby, yes. Great thinking. Hey, Toby?'

I was staring at Rahul, my mind a thousand miles away.

'Toby?' Rahul was looking at me. 'What's got into you?'

'What did you just say, Rahul?' I asked, a grin spreading across my face.

'I don't know,' he replied. 'Something about it being almost as good as being there.'

Suddenly I was aware of Jay, Scott and a few others listening in to our conversation.

'Then let's go there,' I laughed at him. 'I'll take you to Madras.'

'I think the game might have finished by the time you get there, Toby,' Scott said to me.

I kept smiling. 'Trust me, Rahul. It can be done. I'll bring you back a memento, Scott,' I said, without being quite sure why I was saying it.

'Toby, are you okay?' Rahul asked me, puzzled.

'Come round after school, Wednesday night. Okay?'

'Sure. Maybe we can plan that interview, yes?'

Excitement was bubbling up inside me, but I didn't carry on with the conversation. It was enough to know that I had this power, this knowledge, this extraordinary gift that none of the other kids in the library had any idea about.

And the more I tried to explain it or tried to make them believe it, the more stupid it would seem. I had the best secret in the world and I would reveal it in my own time.

Tuesday — afternoon

The next night at training, Mr Pasquali chatted to us at the start of the session. But it wasn't about last Saturday's game, or about how he wanted the practice to go that evening. Instead, he explained that Martian would not be playing with us for a while and that the keeping duties would be taken over by Ally McCabe. We wondered how bad Ivo's injuries were, but Mr Pasquali told us to concentrate on our practice.

Mr Pasquali worked us through another centre-wicket practice during the session. We all had plenty of bowling and fielding to do. Ally stayed behind the stumps all the time we were out there. She was good, too. She was very quick to pick up the direction of the ball and was clean with her glove work — hardly ever dropping the ball. The only problem she seemed to have was if the batter got in the way when the ball came down the leg side. She was willing to listen to suggestions from Mr Pasquali — and from some of the players, too. Best of all, she seemed to be really enjoying it.

Luckily, I was able to avoid Scott for most of the session, though he put me away for a couple of big fours near the end. I hoped that might have got the anger out of his system. Time would tell.

At the end of practice Mr Pasquali brought us all back into a close group.

He must have heard all of us talking about Martian. 'As I told you, Ivo is going to be okay, but he won't be with us for quite some time.'

Everyone started asking questions, but Mr Pasquali held up a hand.

'I know you are all concerned. But Ivo's mum has told me that everything is going to be fine.'

The mood of the afternoon had changed as we gathered up our gear and packed it away. I noticed Mr Pasquali talking with Ally. A moment later she approached me.

'Hey, Toby, can we do a bit of work together? Your bowling was a bit hard to read, you know?'

'It was?'

'Yeah, sometimes it swung one way, sometimes the other.'

'Cool. That's good to hear. Okay, Ally, sure. You want to meet in the gym sometime, then?'

'Yep. I'll see if I can book it for some time next week. I'll let you know.'

We all hung around for a bit, chatting about Ivo.

'You reckon we should just go in and see him?' Jay asked.

'Better ring up first,' I suggested.

'Poor Ivo. He always seems to be the one who gets knocked about. Remember last year he broke his arm and he had those pins inserted in it?' Georgie shook her head.

'My dad often talks about fate and luck.'

We all looked at Rahul.

'That's a bit deep, Rahul,' Ally said.

'Yeah, well I'll ring him soon,' I told them.

Wednesday — afternoon

Mum took Rahul and me into the MCC library again after school the following day. She dropped us off outside the front and told us that she would collect us in exactly an hour. We waved goodbye and raced off to the entrance.

I was excited, that was for sure, but I was also working hard to keep a lid on it. So far, only Georgie had an inkling of what was going on. It was a secret, and I wanted to share it. But I wanted to protect the secret from people I didn't trust. Rahul, I thought, was someone I could trust.

It was spooky to think that maybe the next time I hopped in Mum's car, I could have been to India and back. And what was even more spooky, travelled in time to get there!

When we arrived at the library there was a man working at a computer on the far side, obviously the librarian, and another man with glasses, sitting at the big oval table reading. It was the same guy we had seen last time. Maybe he worked here too. If he did, it sure wasn't too tough a job.

There was no sign of Jim, and no one looked up when we walked in.

'Rahul, come with me. I want to show you something.'

I found the 1987 *Wisden* on the shelf and walked over to the secret door in the wall. I pushed the door open and we went out into the corridor.

Rahul was a few metres behind me and looking doubtful. 'Toby, where are you going?'

'You'll find out in a minute, okay?' I turned to the contents pages at the start. For some reason I could read these. But I couldn't find the right section. 'When did you say that tied Test was again?'

'1986.'

'That's weird. How come it's not in the 1987 *Wisden*?'

'Probably because it was later in the year, September. You need the next year's book, I think. Can we go back inside now?'

Maybe this wasn't meant to happen after all, I thought. But when we got back into the library I got a big shock. There, on the oval table, was a copy of the 1988 *Wisden*. I looked around, but no one seemed to be paying us the slightest bit of attention. Maybe it had been left by the guy with the glasses. He'd closed his book and his head had slumped forward onto his chest.

I picked up the 1988 *Wisden* and headed over to the far side of the library. Rahul followed.

'Okay, Rahul, hold on.'

Maybe I should have thought a bit more about what I was about to do. Maybe I should have thought about the fact that Jim had expressly forbidden me to take anyone. Carrying, as Jim called it. But in the excitement of trying to impress Rahul, who always seemed so much in control, none of these thoughts entered my mind.

I grabbed Rahul's arm, and dragged him closer. I was holding the precious book in my other hand and trying to scan down the contents page.

There it was, clear as day: 'The Australians in India, 1986–87'. I flipped chunks of pages till I got close to the correct page. The numbers in the top corner of each page were becoming clearer.

I knew I had to be quick, or Rahul would drag me back.

'Toby!' he hissed at me. 'What are you doing? Why can't we look at the book at the big table over there, like normal people?'

I got to page 920 then flicked on a few more pages, trying to focus on the headings at the top. I didn't know exactly what page the Test would be on. 'Rahul, was the tie in the first Test match?'

'Yes. Can I see?'

I had a thought. 'Good idea. You find the correct page, then give it to me.'

Everything was racing. I didn't have time to think about what I was doing. Maybe it wouldn't work. Maybe I needed Jim here, with his magical powers. My heart was thumping. I would just give Rahul a taste. Just prove to him that we could go there. Go anywhere! It would be so exciting to show someone else. Especially Rahul. He would be amazed.

He passed the book back to me. I stared with total concentration at the top of the page. I could just make out the word India in a swirly mix of white and black. Rahul was close by.

'India,' I said quietly, staring at the word as it materialised into letters.

There was a gentle knocking, thudding noise going on somewhere in my head. I grabbed Rahul's wrist. The thudding turned to a roar; to a great, whooshing rush of what sounded like air and water surging through my head. I could hear Rahul talking about how useful the match report would be for his project, when suddenly he seemed to stop in mid-sentence.

I opened my eyes. It was as if we were standing in an oven. The heat was amazing. It wasn't just heat; it was sticky, dense heat that squeezed at you from all sides. And there was a terrible smell of really gross toilets. For a moment I thought I was going to be sick.

Beside me Rahul gasped and fell to his knees.

'Rahul,' I cried. 'Get up!'

Slowly he struggled to his feet.

'Wh — what?' he stammered.

We had arrived a little behind the crowd. We were inside the ground but couldn't see the oval. It was like last time. I knew, without knowing exactly why, that we had arrived without anyone knowing. Somehow that seemed important.

Taking him by the shoulders, I forced Rahul to look at me. He wasn't looking too good.

'Rahul, as soon as you've got over being totally freaked out by what's happened, the sooner we can get a look at the game. Okay?'

I was giving it to him straight up. He stared back at me, his eyes not blinking.

'We are in India,' Rahul whispered.

It was more a statement than a question, but I answered anyway.

'Correct.'

'In the year —,' Rahul looked at me.

'1986.'

'I'm not even born yet.'

'Well, that's debatable. I can see you.'

'My mother is alive in this city somewhere. My father too,' Rahul said.

'Yeah, well, let's take a quick look at the cricket. Then we'll head back, okay? Rahul?'

But Rahul looked as if he had other things on his mind.

The noise and the heat closed in around us. Men wearing really long shirts streamed past us, kicking up dust that stung my eyes. There was a dull roar coming from near the oval and an amazing mixture of smells. Half the crowd seemed to be behind the stand here, with us. Everyone was babbling, shouting, pushing and hurrying.

'It's time to go, Rahul. C'mon. Let's move away from here.'

I grabbed him by the arm and dragged him in the opposite direction to the people rushing at us till we were near a fence. Rahul was resisting. At this rate we weren't even going to see any cricket.

'Listen!' I yelled. 'I'm not supposed to do this with someone else.'

I was beginning to worry about having Rahul here with me, especially with Jim's warning about not taking anyone else with me. And Rahul was not looking himself.

'We have to go back. *Now!*'

But Rahul was in another world. He was looking at me as though I wasn't there. Maybe he was thinking of his family. Then I realised that I didn't have the poem on me. I looked around, in absolute panic.

I checked all my pockets, but all I could feel was the little card old Jim had given me for getting into the library.

A large man in what looked like a police uniform was striding towards us.

I closed my eyes and tried to picture the poem. But the only word I could remember was 'dead'.

The man was getting closer. He had a long stick dangling down the side of one leg.

Something about lives being broken, and respecting the gift.

The man stopped in front of us and spoke to Rahul. I couldn't understand what he was saying but Rahul replied, presumably in the same language.

Now there was a horrible stench in the air that had overpowered all the other smells. The heat was beginning to get to me. I was sweating like anything and finding it hard to breathe. My jeans were sticking to me. Desperately, I dipped into my front pocket and pulled out the card.

The man was nodding at me and waving an arm at Rahul.

I turned the card over. Relief flooded through me as I saw two neat lines of handwriting across the back that I hadn't known were there. I had never turned the card over before.

I turned to see the policeman shaking his head, pointing at me and then at the ground.

He made a final comment and walked away. Rahul was starting to sit down.

Again, I grabbed him by the arm, and without even asking him what they'd been talking about, I read aloud the two lines on the card.

Now, hide your home, your age, your soul
To roam this place and seek your goal.

The last word had hardly left my lips when the roaring inside my head started again, though not quite as loudly as before. I was aware of us leaving the heat and the smell behind. I tried to keep my eyes open, but it was impossible — like when you sneeze. It only took a moment, but I knew that we had gone. And that the going and the arriving were split by a second, no more.

The first Test match played over five days took place in Sydney, during February 1892. This was also the first time 6 balls were bowled in each over. In all the Tests before 1892, overs were just 4 balls long.

9 The Heat

'WHAT the heck do you two think you're playing at?'

I looked up at the librarian. 'You won't find anything down there on the floor. Now hop it back to the table. Don't kids nowadays use tables to do their work on? Eh?' He was shaking his head as he headed back inside and over to his computer.

Luckily he hadn't seen the *Wisden*, which was lying on the floor, half underneath me. I watched him walk off, grabbed the *Wisden*, and hauled Rahul to his feet. We walked back to the oval table as calmly as we could. The man with the glasses had gone.

Rahul hadn't said a word. I looked at him. He looked pale and worn out.

'Rahul? Speak to me.'

He turned to me slowly, a smile beginning to take shape.

'We have to go back again, you know. When can we go? I'll get some things together then you can take me back, okay?'

78

It was as if something or someone had taken over Rahul's thinking. He wasn't sounding like his normal, controlled self.

'Not yet. Not until I talk to Jim,' I whispered and told him all about Jim and our shared gift.

'Right. Okay. Sorry. Where is he, then?'

'I'm not sure. Leave it with me though, okay?'

Rahul looked at me closely.

'Toby? What on earth just happened?' A drop of sweat fell from my forehead and landed on the table next to the *Wisden* book. 'We've just been to India. It was hot, wasn't it?'

We looked at the tiny splash of sweat on the table.

Wonderingly, Rahul touched it with a finger.

'Sweat from India,' he said.

We stayed for another 20 minutes or so. Rahul jotted down notes from the books in front of him, while I sat in a daze. I couldn't believe he could have suddenly become so calm, sitting there quietly, going from book to notepad as if nothing had happened.

Just before we left, the librarian came over to see how we were getting on.

'Where's Jim today?' I asked him.

'Jim's not very well at the moment, I'm afraid.'

'Could you tell me where he is? I'd like to send him a get well card.'

The librarian seemed a bit surprised. 'Well, that's a nice thought. If you send it care of the Simpson Hospital I'm sure he'll get it.'

'Okay, thanks,' I said, getting up.

'You boys come back any time.'

'Sure. Thanks.'

I headed across to the secret door.

'But maybe using the normal door,' he added, smiling at us. We paused. 'No, no, go on. It's our secret, okay?' He chuckled.

Thursday — afternoon

Scott Craven was his usual self at practice the following day. Rahul was quiet, though I didn't think he'd go rushing about, telling everyone of his encounter with an Indian policeman nearly 20 years ago!

'Here, I'm sure Toby would have forgotten your memento of Madras, but I didn't,' he told Scott.

Before I could say anything, Rahul had reached into his pocket and pulled out a couple of pebbles. I stared at them, then held out a hand to take a close look.

'You sure you didn't take them out of your brain?' Scott reached over, grabbed the small stones and hurled them onto the dirt road by the nets.

'You're weird,' Scott said to us.

He scowled. A moment later he wandered off, cursing and muttering under his breath.

At practice I got Mr Pasquali to toss ball after ball at me as he watched me play down the line. He called it a 'V'. I really didn't need a helmet or gloves, because he was throwing them pitched up and making me play forward defensive shots. But he insisted that we should duplicate real batting conditions as often as we could.

Later, a few of us went to the centre-wicket and bowled to Ally. There was no batter, just a set of stumps for us to aim at. After a while, Ally didn't bother replacing the bails on the stumps.

She moved quickly into position and took each ball neatly. I showed her how I held the ball to get it to swing the way I wanted to.

'So that's why you guys work so hard at keeping one side of the ball shiny?' she asked me.

'Yep. We also try to keep it off the ground when it's being thrown back to the bowler.'

Ally looked at me questioningly.

'The more the ball stays off the ground, the longer you can keep the shine on it.'

'Okay, so don't roll it up to, what do you call them, middle-off or something?'

'Mid-off and mid-on. No. Well of course it doesn't matter when Scott's bowling.'

Ally laughed.

'I guess you don't have that problem to worry about in a softball game?' I asked.

'Nope — I'm sort of missing its simpleness, though, compared with cricket.'

'But are you enjoying wicket keeping? Oh yeah, until Martian comes back, that is.' I added quickly.

We worked on a little leg-side trap, where I sent a slightly quicker ball, after a few slower ones, down outside the leg stump. After a few goes, we both had it working well. Ally called it our 'TLT' — Toby's leg trap. I told her that if I pointed to the covers, there would be a TLT on, next ball.

'Okay, so if you see me point to covers, come up and stand behind the stumps. I'll bowl two slower ones outside the off-stump, then the third one will be a bit quicker down outside his pads. If the batter is out of his crease, you whip the bails off after you've caught the ball. Actually, whip them off anyway, it's good practice.'

We practised the TLT a few times and it wasn't long before Ally was taking the ball cleanly and in one easy movement swiping the bails off the stumps.

'All we need is a batter,' I called to her.

'Bring him on!'

I noticed Scott Craven wander off in the last few minutes of practice. Jay had also gone, and he wasn't looking happy when he returned a few minutes later.

Georgie noticed that Jay wasn't his usual cheerful self, too. Maybe she'd seen them head off together.

'Did Scott do anything?' Georgie asked him, as we were packing up the gear.

'Nah, didn't even see him.'

'Oh, it's just that I saw the two of you heading off together and I wondered.'

Jay didn't look up from the pads that he was putting into pairs. I wasn't convinced about his answer. Georgie and I exchanged glances.

'By the way,' she said, 'I asked Mr Pasquali about Ivo. He said that Mrs Marshall hadn't wanted him to make a fuss, but if anyone asked, he could tell them Ivo was at the Simpson, and we could see him. But we've gotta ring first.'

'The Simpson!' I wheeled round.

'Yeah. Why, what's the matter? You had some bad experience there, or something?'

'Georgie, that's where Jim Oldfield is. You know, the guy at the library.'

'Great. Maybe I can fetch him another glass of water.'

BOWLING

It is important to try to keep the shine on one side of the ball for as long as possible. If one side of the ball is shiny, there is more chance that the ball will swing, as air will move across each side of the ball at different speeds, causing it to move. This makes the job for the batter more difficult. This is why it's important to try to keep the ball off the ground as much as possible when passing it back to the bowler for the next delivery.

The highest partnership in a one-day international was made by Rahul Dravid (153) and Sachin Tendulkar (186) against New Zealand on 8 November 1999. The two added 331 runs for the second wicket. India's score for the game was 2/376.

10 The Warning

I logged into the CROC room, expecting a few others to be there.

Georgie: hey, who's here
Toby: just got on, you still here, georgie?
Rahul: thought you'd never get here, toby
Toby: hi rahul
Rahul: evening all, toby, are we on for fri?
Jay: i'm here to
Georgie: jay — thought you were out tonight?
Jay: i'm aloud to change my mind, are'nt i

Suddenly I knew it wasn't Jay. He was the best speller in the class, by a mile. My mind jumped back to when Georgie had seen Scott following Jay near the end of practice.

Georgie: hey toby, i've told rahul all about jim and
            everything, hope that's okay

Rahul: I can't wait to meet him myself, toby

Toby: maybe now's not the best time

Jay: no, tell

Georgie: go on toby, you're dying to

Rahul: careful everyone, this is major deep, how
            much do you know, georgie?

Georgie: only that there's this nice (I think) old guy at
            the library at the mcg who has given toby an
            awesome poem and is telling him weird
            stories about travelling through time and
            stuff. it's cool

Rahul: what do you know, jay?

Toby: yeah, tell us what you think, jay. tell us what
            happened in the library when we first met
            jim

Georgie: jay — you there?

Rahul: he's gone

Toby: no he hasn't, he's watching us and reading
            it all

Jay: your a pack of sicko loosers

Toby: get out of the room everyone, now

There was no more conversation. I rang up Georgie,
then Rahul, explaining my suspicion. They both
agreed that there was only one solution. We would
have to dump that room and create another. The
problem was, would we include Jay? Was it his fault?
Or did Scott bully the information out of him?

Sometimes Georgie wrote by just putting down on
paper the first things that came into her head. I tried

it myself. I took out a pen and some paper, sat down at my desk, and started writing.

○ *I have travelled to different parts of the world, and to different times, and only Jim knows.*
○ *Except for Rahul, who went all freaky when it happened to him.*
○ *And Georgie, who sort of knows something weird is going on.*
○ *And I should tell Jay — after all, he is one of my best friends.*
○ *Ivo is in hospital, obviously pretty sick.*
○ *Jim is there too.*
○ *Jimbo isn't allowed to play cricket.*
○ *Georgie, and the kiss comment.*
○ *Scott is out to get me, for running him out.*
○ *Scott has got to Jay, and logged into CROC and now must surely know there is something big happening that he isn't a part of.*

The answer never did come to me. Maybe I just needed to share this whole thing with someone — an adult. But something was holding me back.

There was a tap at the door. Mum came in.

'Hey, kiddo, do you want a snack? Dad's making pancakes. He needs some eaters!'

'Sure, Mum, coming,' I said.

I wasn't that hungry, but I went to the kitchen anyway. Mum had got out the family videos, and there were Nat, my younger sister, and me, prancing

86

about, opening presents and looking cute and cuddly. It was good to forget about things for a while.

Then, suddenly I thought — if there was a game of cricket happening at the MCG that day, the day my sister and I were messing about in our little backyard pool all those years ago, I could travel back in time with the correct *Wisden* book, walk from the cricket ground, sneak up to the back fence, lean over, and watch myself, aged three, playing in the pool with my sister.

Could I?

Would I?

I knew there was no way I could answer that right now.

In 1884 the captain of an English team forced the touring Australians to show their bats.
He wanted to make sure they were not too wide!

11 The Simpson Hospital

DAD had been fine about visiting Ivo.

'Of course I'll take you,' he said. 'Poor kid. He deserves a change of luck, doesn't he?'

On the way there in the car he shared old cricket stories. 'Did I ever tell you about the time a spectator ran out onto the ground and got tackled?'

'No. Who did the tackling?'

'Terry Alderman, a great fast bowler from Western Australia. Actually, Toby, not unlike you in terms of style. He could swing the ball both ways. There was a great bit of graffiti up during the Ashes tour, '89 I think. "Thatcher out." Then someone had scrawled next to that, "lbw Alderman".'

We both had a chuckle. I had no idea who Thatcher was, but Dad thought it was funny.

'Anyway, this guy got tackled by Terry Alderman and he ended up dislocating his shoulder.'

'Who?'

'Terry Alderman. Absolute disaster. He was out of the game for ages.'

'Dad?'

'Yes Toby?' Dad looked at me. 'What's up?'

It was the closest I'd got, so far, to telling him about the *Wisdens* and the time travel. Dad, of all people, wouldn't freak out. But there was something holding me back.

'Tell me about that Test match between New Zealand and the West Indies. You know, the one when the West Indies were none for 276 and —'

'Ah yes. Amazing game. Probably one of the greatest escapes of all time.'

I decided I would tell him my secret later, and we would go on journey after journey, visiting all the famous games that have been played. We would make a list of them.

Maybe the biggest thing stopping me was the thought of Jim, lying somewhere in a hospital bed. Did he have a family? Was he someone's grandad? I wanted to know a bit more about him. And then, maybe with him, decide what I would do with this magical power I had.

I owed Jim that.

While we were all visiting Martian, I would duck out and try to find him, just to let him know that I hadn't forgotten him. But mainly I just wanted to see him again and make sure he was okay.

Hospitals are quiet and lonely. Well, the parts that most people see are. There's probably plenty more action in the operating theatres, and more noise down in the emergency section, but I didn't want to go and test out that theory.

I was meeting the rest of the guys in the foyer, where Dad said he would wait for me. We made our way up to Ivo's room on the first floor. His parents were with him. Ivo lay propped up on a heap of pillows and there was a drip next to him.

'Does it hurt?' I asked him, looking at the place where the needle must have been passing some solution into his body. His mum smiled at us, and left, with Mr Marshall, saying that she was going to buy some fruit.

Ivo looked at the drip, smiled, and shook his head.

'Thanks for coming, guys,' he said, tears brimming.

'Oh, God, I knew this would happen,' Georgie burst out, starting to cry herself. 'What is it, Ivo?' she asked, between sobs. 'Why are you here?'

Ivo looked at our worried faces.

'Nothing,' he replied, shaking his head. There was a silence. Rahul picked up a clipboard at the end of his bed.

'You going to tell us, Ivo, or am I going to have to find out for myself?' he asked, adjusting his glasses.

'Well, they're doing a few tests and stuff and they did a bit of surgery too. I've just got to stay here a few days till things settle down.'

Georgie recovered, blew her nose, perched herself on the end of the bed and said, 'Ivo, I want to tell you that you're the number one keeper in our team, and that as soon as you're back you're going straight to the keeper's spot. Okay?'

'Sure, George. You bet.'

'Yep. If that doesn't happen, this team is going to lose both its female players.'

'Both?' I asked, looking at her.

'Yep,' she said. 'Absadoodle.'

'Well I don't think I'll be pushing for selection for a few weeks yet,' said Ivo.

We told him about the game against St Mary's and me running Craven out.

I caught Georgie's eye and nodded to the door. She shook her head.

'I'm just going to duck out for a moment, okay, guys?'

I didn't wait for a reply. I walked over to the nurses' area and asked the man there where Jim Oldfield was. He clicked his mouse and looked at his screen.

'Room 225. Up another floor. Are you a relative?'

'I'm sort of his godson. My dad's just gone to buy some fruit,' I added, as an afterthought.

He shrugged, and went back to his work.

* * *

I tapped on the door. There was no reply. I eased it open and poked my head around the corner. There were two beds. Two old men lay asleep. Jim was by the window. There was a cricket book on his bedside table.

I walked over and looked down at him. He lay very still. For a panic-stricken moment I thought he was dead.

Then he opened his eyes.

'It's all right, Toby. I'm a light sleeper,' he whispered, smiling. 'It was good of you to come.' He sounded as though he was expecting me.

'That's okay, Mr Oldfield.'

He turned his head towards me. 'Jim,' he said. 'Remember?'

'Yes. Jim. Of course. I've travelled again,' I blurted out. 'I know I shouldn't have, but I did. And I took Rahul with me to India. It was scary. It was —'

'Ssh,' Jim whispered, looking over at the other person. 'I know you did, Toby. And I hope you have learnt a valuable lesson. Those you carry are prone to go against your will. Against the will of the poem. Did this boy want to stay? Did he make it hard for you?'

'Yes,' I whispered back, 'he did. It was like he was destined to be there, or something.'

'What did you say his name was?'

'Rahul.'

'Of Indian descent?'

'Yes,' I replied.

'Then he had other ties that are very hard to work

92

against. He is one who perhaps should not travel with you, Toby.'

I had heaps of questions to ask Jim, but now that I was here they stuck in my throat.

'Why are you here, Jim? Are you okay?'

'My heart is not what it used to be, and it's playing up just at the time when a certain special boy has come into my life,' he replied.

'Do you mean me?' I asked. 'I should never have walked into that library.'

'Ah, but you had to. Don't you see?'

I didn't. Not one bit.

'Jim, are you in danger?' I asked, fearing his answer.

'Not while I'm here, Toby. No, not at all,' he added, sensing my anxiety.

'But, why did I —'

A nurse walked in and started shooing me off as if I were a dog or something.

'Please,' Jim protested, rising slightly from his pillows. 'He is my only family.' He slumped back down again.

'And where's your mother?' the nurse asked me as she straightened Jim's bedclothes.

'Dad's just out buying some fruit,' I told her. I might as well have just announced the fact over the loudspeaker system. I seemed to be telling everyone what Ivo's dad was doing.

'Right, then. Visiting time's over. You can come back tomorrow.'

Old Jim reached out a hand. It was dry and lumpy, with veins and other marks. I reached over and took it. He clasped my hands in his.

'Re-read the poem tonight, Toby. Promise me you will do that?'

'I'll read it, Jim. I promise,' I said quietly.

He lay back and sighed. He looked content. Then he mumbled something. I didn't quite catch what he said.

'Pardon? What was that?'

But he just smiled, and shook his head.

I stayed a moment longer, looking at his wrinkled, gentle face. Then I turned around and left.

Jack Gregory, playing for Australia, holds the record for the most catches (by a non-wicket keeper) taken in a series. He took 15 catches during the 5 matches Australia played against England in 1921.

12 The Visit

Saturday — morning

I was running late for the game and this time it was Dad who was sitting in the car waiting for me. I couldn't find my gloves. Nat had been belting some forehands at me and I'd put them on to protect my fingers. I eventually found them outside, under the trampoline. There were a few teeth marks in the soft, padded bits that go over the fingers but they were okay.

I grabbed the gloves and raced out to the car.

'You going to use anything else to bat with?' Dad asked, as I slammed the door and started to buckle up.

'What?' I said, looking at him blankly.

'Your cricket bag!'

'Oh yeah!'

Dad just chuckled to himself and turned the radio up as I raced back inside.

As expected, Scott Craven denied being online the night before last.

'Why would I want to do that stupid chat stuff? With you?' he scoffed, spinning his bat through his hands. Jay wasn't talking to anyone.

It was much cooler this Saturday. We jogged out for a warm-up, with Mr Pasquali hitting us some short, and then longer catches. No one was really too concerned about defending such a huge total. The highest score we'd made was 271, and with Scott measuring out his long run, I didn't think there was any way St Mary's would get near it.

Once again Scott was in the action, taking 3 wickets himself and a catch at point. I stood next to Ally in first slip, answering all her questions and giving her hints about what to do after the ball had been played. She certainly seemed to be picking it up quickly.

I was brought on to bowl when they were 5 for 72. My first 2 overs were maidens. Scott Craven was itching to get back on and clean up the rest of the batting.

'One more over,' Jono said to me, 'or two, if you get a wicket.' I nodded. I bowled the first three balls a bit slower, pitching them just outside off-stump, trying to entice the batter to come out of his crease. Ally had moved forward and was standing just behind the stumps — as she would for a spin bowler. The batter pushed forward again on the third ball, but only managed to pad it back down the pitch. I looked at Ally, then pointed out to the covers.

'You want me to move or what?' Scott yelled. 'Whaddya pointing at me for?' I waved for him to come in a few metres. He walked in about five, looking at Jono, our captain, as he did so. Jono nodded.

I got to the end of my run-up, looked up, and nodded at Ally. She nodded back. I noticed her move, just slightly, towards the leg side.

But the ball, which was meant to race down the leg side, ended up more on middle and leg-stump. Again the batter pushed forward, but in trying to turn the ball to the leg side, it spooned out to short cover, having caught a leading edge. Scott raced in a couple of metres and dived forward to take the catch.

I clapped my hands, shrugged my shoulders at Ally and walked over to Scott.

'Nice work, Toby,' Jono said to me. 'You can take over all fielding positions!'

'Great catch,' I said to Scott. He tossed the ball back to me with a look that was almost friendly. I think he was impressed with my decision to move him in.

'We won't tell anyone about TLT yet, eh, Toby?' Ally laughed at the end of the over.

'No, maybe not,' I replied.

I got my extra over, and was whacked for two fours and two singles. Still, the wicket was worth it.

We won by 111 runs. Before we left, Mr Pasquali reminded us that next week's game, a one-dayer against the Scorpions, the top team on the ladder, was the big one.

I caught up with Jay as he was walking across to his family's car.

'Hello, Jay!'

'Hi,' he said, in a flat voice.

I got straight to the point.

'Jay, you shouldn't have given Scott your ID for CROC. I reckon —'

'I couldn't help it. He threatened me. He said he was going to hurt you big time because of the run-out if I didn't tell him what was going on, you know, with all the stuff happening.'

'So you gave him your ID and told him to find out for himself?' I said.

'I was protecting you, okay!' he said, sounding annoyed.

'Okay. Fair enough. I would've probably done the same thing too.'

'I know there's something weird going on, that's all.'

'Yeah, but do you want to know about it?' I asked.

Jay didn't reply.

'Were you in CROC last night?' I asked him, my voice quieter.

'Nope. I couldn't get on. Craven must have been waiting for you guys for ages. What happened?'

'He can't spell like you can.'

Jay looked up at last and smiled.

'I was kind of hoping something like that might happen,' he said. 'Are you going to tell me what this is all about?'

I felt a bit bad that Jay didn't know, like Rahul or Georgie and even Jimbo, and I at least owed him an explanation. After all, he was the one that I'd dragged back to the library during the excursion.

'Of course. Come round this arvo and I'll tell you then. I've also been thinking for a while about going to visit Jimbo, you want to do that?'

'Jimbo?' He looked surprised. 'You sure?'

'Yeah, why?'

'I dunno. It's just, well, I don't reckon Jimbo would have many visitors.' Jay looked anxious.

'Well, maybe we'll be the first. Okay?'

'Yeah, okay.'

But he didn't sound convinced.

We got there about mid-afternoon. I was hoping they'd be watching the one-dayer on TV. But then I remembered that Jimbo's Saturdays were reserved for garage cleaning.

Jimbo's dad met us at the door.

'Yes?' he asked. He was holding a pair of glasses in his hands and rubbing his eyes.

'Um, is Jimbo in?' I asked.

'He's busy right now. Sorry.' He started to close the door.

'Well could we come back later?' I tried to sound cheerful. I didn't feel it.

Another voice, maybe his mum's, was calling out somewhere inside the house.

'Who is it?'

'We were just wondering whether we could see Jimbo,' I called into the darkness.

We stood there for a moment, a bit confused.

'Here to see Jimbo, did you say?' Jimbo's mum stood at the door wearing a pair of jeans and a shirt way too big for her. She looked sort of neat and trendy. She had a mobile phone in one hand, and it was pressed to her stomach. She was obviously on a call. She was smiling.

Boy, this was like major security.

'We're not armed,' Jay whispered under his breath. I nudged him.

Jimbo's mum came out onto the porch and looked at us closely, as if she'd never seen kids before.

'Well you'd better come in,' she said finally.

'He's not busy?' Jay asked, with a trace of sarcasm.

'Jimbo? He's always busy. Jimbo! There are some friends here to see you. Jimbo!' she called.

The first thing I noticed, lying in the hallway, was a cricket kit, an old-looking one, along with a whole range of other stuff, lined up along the walls.

Jimbo's dad saw me looking at the stuff and said, 'Garage sale. We're getting rid of a whole pile of junk.' He kicked the kit. Jimbo had also appeared. He looked surprised to see us.

'Toby. Jay. Hi there.'

'Hi, Jimbo.'

'You can't be interested in that old stuff,' his dad said, seeing me still staring at the old off-white cricket bag. The initials R.T. could just be made out on the front.

'Come through,' said Jimbo. We walked up a wide flight of stairs and into his bedroom. It was massive. It was like his own living room with a huge bed, a desk, computer with all the attachments, bookcases stacked with books and a couple of big, wooden chests. Probably filled with interesting stuff. He noticed me looking around.

'I guess being an only child has its benefits,' he smiled. 'So, what brings you two here?'

'Well, actually, I suppose I, well ... we, really want to know why you can't play in the cricket team.'

'Even though you can make it to training,' Jay added.

Jimbo didn't speak.

'Well, most nights you can make it to training,' I said.

'Yeah, except for Thursday night,' said Jay. We were blabbering.

Jimbo sat on the bed, picked up a cricket ball and started spinning it in the air. He looked at the door, raised his eyes and nodded in that direction. I went over and closed it.

'And, if I tell you, then you'll go?' he asked us.

'Sure,' I said. 'You really don't want us here, do you?'

'Do you want to be here?'

'Yes. We came to see you,' I replied.

He paused for a moment, then caught the ball and held it.

'Well, the reason I don't play is that my father won't let me. I'm allowed to train three nights a fortnight, but I'm not allowed to play in any games.'

I was shocked.

'Why?' Jay asked.

Jimbo shrugged and shook his head. 'Dad had a bad experience playing the game himself. It turned him off. He vowed on that day that he would never play again. It looks like his vow has extended to me.'

'But can't you tell him that his problems are nothing to do with you? This is your life. What the —'

Jimbo was looking at me impatiently.

'It's not your problem, Toby, but thanks for your concern.' He was about to say something else, then stopped.

'What?' Jay asked.

'Well, since you're both so interested, there is one other factor. I won't mention any names, but someone you know is also involved, indirectly.'

Jimbo wasn't making sense.

'Come again?' I said.

'Dad played against one of the fathers of the current team,' he told us.

'And that was his bad experience?' I asked.

'You'd better go, guys. I've got heaps to do.'

'But it's Saturday, Jimbo!' exclaimed Jay, struggling to stay calm.

'Unless it's your cricket project,' I offered.

'No such luck. Can't do that at home, either.'

'Sounds like cricket doesn't get much of a look in at your house,' I said.

'So how come you've got a cricket ball in your hand?' Jay asked.

'Mr Pasquali lent it to me one night after practice. Dad doesn't know I've got it.'

'C'mon, let's go,' Jay said, walking towards the door.

'Well, see you round, Jimbo,' I called.

'You will. See ya, guys.'

'Weird,' Jay muttered. I was inclined to agree with him, and wondered what it was all about.

'There's something sort of different about Jimbo, isn't there?' Jay said to me as we grabbed our bikes.

'I like him, but I know what you mean. I wish there was something we could do, you know, to get him to play cricket with us.'

'What, like talk to his dad?'

'Dunno. Maybe. I wonder if his dad knows just how awesome a cricketer Jimbo is.'

'My dad would be over the moon if I was even half as good,' Jay said, racing off ahead of me.

I clipped my helmet on and pedalled after him.

FIELDING — READY FOR A CATCH

You can be sure that the one chance you get to take a catch — because they don't come that often — will be the time when you weren't as ready as you should have been. To give yourself the best chance of taking a catch, here are a few tips.

Walk in with the bowler, if you are not fielding in a catching position — in other words, if you're not too close to the batter. This alerts you to the fact that a ball is about to be bowled, has you leaning forward, anticipating and on the move. Watch the batter. After the delivery, use the few moments you have to relax, but be on the lookout for any weaknesses in the batter that you can pass on to the bowler or captain.

When taking a catch, the most important thing to remember is to keep your eyes on the ball. Try to get your body into position as early as possible so you can focus on actually taking the catch.

For outfield catches, make sure your fingers are pointing either up or down, so the ball will come to rest safely in the palms of your hands.

For close-in catches, the fingers should be pointing down for balls that come below waist height, and up for those that come at you higher.

Stay relaxed, and keep your hands 'soft'.

One last point. You've got to want the ball to come your way. So if you don't like the feel of a cricket ball, buy one and get to like it. Toss it to yourself. Make the throws higher and higher. Catch 10 out of 10. Then get a friend to toss you more.

Then more, at different heights and speeds. Then more.

A monster innings was completed by a batsman in Tasmania in 1902. Charles Eady smashed a huge 566 runs for his club team, Break o'Day. He made the score over three afternoons, and hit 13 fives (that's what six used to be worth) and a cool 68 fours. On the first day of the game, Eady took 7/87. I wonder if he was man of the match!

13 The Garage

Sunday — morning

GEORGIE came round the next day. She found me out in the garage, earning a bit of pocket money by cleaning the place up. I had stumbled across a box full of Dad's books, and when she walked in I had just pulled out the find of the century — a couple of old *Wisdens*.

I looked up sharply as her shadow loomed over me. It was a spooky moment, especially as I was about to open one of the *Wisdens*.

'You can't keep your hands off those old books,' she said, striding into the dimness.

'Look!' I said, holding up another three books.

'Great! Let's spend the rest of the afternoon sitting here in the dust reading them.'

'Really? You mean it?' Then I saw her face. She didn't mean it.

'Anyway,' she went on, 'your dad said I'm not to

distract you from the cleaning, and since I'm not too keen on helping, I'm going inside to write.'

'Okay. We'll make a new CROC site when I come in. Won't be long.'

'Cool,' she called as she slipped away.

I settled myself comfortably on the box of books, and opened the *Wisden* at the contents page. I knew what I was searching for. I had noticed the year when Jim had pulled down the *Wisden* to search for Dad's game. It was the obvious choice and a fantastic chance to try another time travel trip.

Would it work from the garage? Could I use *Wisdens* that weren't from the MCC library?

I searched down until I came to a line that said Overseas Domestic Cricket. It was getting easier for me to navigate my way through the sections, trying to focus on the team names when they appeared.

Soon I sensed the rushing, swirling noises in my head as the names of the teams became clear. I had to turn away quickly, because the game turned out to be a Victoria–Western Australia match. A few pages on, though, it happened. The words Victoria and South Australia dissolved, then became clearer. I glanced down the page. There was a paragraph of writing and then the scorecard itself. It was impossible to focus on. The writing was small and the blur was making my eyes sore.

I dragged my eyes back to the top of the page. I was getting better at it. The whooshing in my head suddenly went quiet. I opened my eyes. There was a shout from somewhere to my left.

I was sitting in an empty part of one of the huge stands at the MCG. For a moment I just sat, hardly daring to breathe. The shout I'd heard was from a man who, along with a sprinkling of spectators around the ground, was applauding the fact that someone had just taken a wicket.

I looked up at the scoreboard. It wasn't the electronic one I was used to. It was an enormous black box with all the players' names. My eyes raced across it looking for Jones. And there it was: P. Jones. There were no numbers next to his name, as there were with some of the others. Dad hadn't had a bowl yet.

Then the realisation of where I was and who I was looking at hit me like a train. I wanted to jump and scream 'Dad!' and run out and say, 'Hi!'. It was the weirdest feeling to be looking at my dad, and yet he wasn't my dad. Not yet, anyway.

I walked down to the fence. It was hard to tell who Dad was. I could rule out the bowler and keeper. I should have asked him what position he fielded in. Maybe he would have forgotten. Maybe I'd be able to jog his memory when I saw him next.

I wasn't nervous any more. As long as I travelled alone, it seemed easy enough to return. So I thought I would spend a bit longer here, exploring, and at least getting a good look at Dad, the cricketer.

And then I had another thought. Why not go and look at the old library while I was here?

I settled down to watch the match. I noticed that a little light went on next to the player's name when he fielded the ball. It took a few overs, and I had eliminated most of the players by their build and looks anyway, but finally, out at mid-on, Dad stopped a full-blooded on-drive. He didn't field it cleanly, and he spent the next few minutes shaking and looking at his hand. He got a good clap from his team-mates. I clapped pretty hard too.

'Way to go, Dad!' I yelled, before I'd had time to think about how stupid I was for saying it. A couple of heads turned to look at me.

A short time later the players left the field for a break. It was the perfect opportunity for me to visit the library. I had to leave the stand and walk around outside the ground itself, to get to the other side.

I used the little ticket I was given to get back into the ground, but a man wearing a blue coat stopped me from going into the Members' section.

He was staring at me. Or, more exactly, at my shorts.

'You'll be pulling them up then, young feller?' he said, frowning slightly.

I gave them a tug, but they slipped straight back down again. I took my baseball cap off before he made a comment about that too.

'Hand-me-downs, eh?' he chuckled. 'You need a belt, lad.'

'My dad's playing,' I explained to him, trying to change the subject.

'Oh, is he? And who might that be?'

'Peter Jones,' I told him. 'He asked me to take a message to Jim Oldfield — in the library,' I added, as an afterthought.

'Well, be quick about it,' he said. The mention of Jim's name seemed to work like magic, even back in this time.

I raced off before he had time to do some quick mental sums and realise that Dad would have to have been about 12 when I was born. Maybe the guy wasn't a keen cricket fan.

The place was only half the size it was the last time I was here. It still felt the same, though. The secret door was still there, and the floorboards creaked as I made my way up the stairs and over to the oval table. I thought there was a whole row of *Wisdens* missing — until I realised that they hadn't been published yet!

I got that shivery, goose-bumpy feeling again as I thought of just where, and when, I was. I wanted to tell someone that P. Jones would make 23 and not take a wicket, and that the Vics would win.

But the lines of the poem, some of them now locked in my memory, reminded me of the dangers of doing that.

> *And never speak and never boast,*
> *And never taunt, nor ever toast ...*

So I walked quietly across the room and spoke to a man standing by a large desk near the card file.

'Is Jim Oldfield around?'

'He's gone to lunch, young feller. Are you his grandson?'

'No.'

'I think he said that he wasn't coming back in this afternoon, too,' the man added. 'Can I give him a message?'

'No, it's okay. Just say that Toby called.'

'Toby. All right then.'

I took a last look at the *Wisdens* and headed back out.

I spent another 15 minutes soaking up the atmosphere of a sunny afternoon, watching the cricket. This time I found a seat a bit further back from the oval itself. I couldn't take my eyes off Dad. He wasn't getting to do much, but every time he fielded the ball I clapped loudly. One time he misfielded. The ball bounced from his shin and the batters stole a run. I felt awful.

I wanted to shout, 'Head up, Dad!', the way he sometimes shouted to me while I was playing sport. Now he was rubbing his shin. No one else was paying him any attention, but I couldn't focus on anyone else.

I watched a couple more overs, then suddenly realised that I had other things I should be doing. I was supposed to be in our garage cleaning it out!

I found a quiet spot — away from the few spectators sprinkled around where I had been sitting — and reeled off a couple of lines of the poem.

Suddenly I was back home. The *Wisden* book I had used was closed and back in its box. For a moment I was worried that somehow time itself had done something weird, and I had returned a day later, or even a week. I glanced at my watch. It was five past five. I raced inside, belted through the kitchen and into the living room. Georgie was watching TV and Dad was reading.

My first thought when I saw Dad was to ask him if his shin still hurt, but I stopped myself just in time. Instead I just stared at him. He wasn't just any old dad — he had just been playing cricket at the MCG!

'Dad!' I called.

He looked up, a bit surprised by the excitement in my voice.

'Hi!' Now Dad and Georgie were both looking at me. 'Sorry I've been so long!' I blurted.

They seemed baffled.

'We've missed you terribly, haven't we Georgie?'

'Oh, terribly,' she said.

'I hear you found some cricket books out there,' Dad remarked. 'They're not very interesting, you know.'

'Oh, I wouldn't say that,' I replied.

The highest number of catches taken by a wicket keeper in a Test match happened in November 1995, when Toby Russell, playing for England against South Africa, took 11 catches. Bob Taylor (England) and Adam Gilchrist (Australia) have each taken 10 catches in a Test match.

14 The Agreement

Monday — morning

RAHUL was fired up about doing the Madras Test for his cricket assignment and, amazingly, had arranged a couple of interviews, as we'd discussed. The teachers were impressed too. They said that it would 'add another dimension to his assignment', whatever that meant.

'I guess that should give you all you need, Rahul,' I said to him, hoping that he had lost interest in getting back to India. No such luck.

'Toby, I have an opportunity to see cricket in my own country. You cannot possibly not take me back. Just once more, I say. Please?'

I shook my head. 'I can't. Jim said something about how tricky it is to take someone with you. How they can make it hard by getting too involved.'

But Rahul wouldn't give up. After he had interviewed Dean Jones, he became even more insistent.

113

'Toby, you wouldn't believe how Dean Jones suffered. I talked to him on the phone.'

'Yeah? What'd he say?'

'That he lost seven kilos from the heat and humidity and that it took him two months to put it back on.'

'Phew, must have been hot.'

'Hot! It was over 40°C, with the humidity at 90 per cent. He couldn't keep any fluid down, but he kept on batting and batting. All through the day. When he was on 170, he told Allan Border, who was batting with him, that he'd had enough. That he was really sick.'

Rahul paused, shaking his head.

'And?'

'Do you know what Border said to him?'

'Course I don't. What did he say?'

'He said, "Okay, I'll get someone tougher to come in".'

'But didn't Dean Jones make over 200?'

'That's just it. He got the message. He stayed out there.'

Rahul was waving around a wad of notes he'd obviously scrawled during his phone conversation with Dean Jones.

'I need to get my notes in order, Toby. I'll tell you more tomorrow.'

Rahul caught up with me the next day, during lunchtime. He was out of control with excitement.

'Toby, I've been thinking carefully about what you

said. And it's true. When we went to Chennai I was just a bit overcome by the whole thing. But I know what to expect now. And I want to give you this.' Rahul pulled a piece of paper out of his pocket and unfolded it. It was a list of points. 'Go on, read it!' he said excitedly.

- Toby is to decide when to do the travel, both to and from Chennai.
- I will not question his decisions.
- Toby is to carry this piece of paper with him while we are in Chennai.
- I will never ask to go again.
- I will tell Scott Craven everything I know about the time travel if I do not go once more.

Signed _____ (Rahul) _____ (Toby)

He looked at me expectantly.

'You wouldn't tell Scott Craven, Rahul?' It was more a statement than a question, but it didn't come out that way.

'Yes I would. I'm very sorry, but I would. This is the opportunity of a lifetime for me. And for you, of course. You can't go to India on your own.'

'Why can't I?'

'Well, for one, you would get lost. You would need someone to help you with the language. With dealing with all the weird situations that can arise in a place like India.'

'Maybe I don't want to go to India.'

'You know what? Dean Jones made 210 for the Aussies. He was throwing up on the field. He was totally exhausted. He was cramping. But he kept on going and going and going. When they finally got him out, he was taken to hospital. Or so they say. But was he? Or is it just a big myth? We can be the first to find out. As soon as I see Dean Jones lying in a hospital bed, then we can come straight home.'

'But didn't you ask him?'

Rahul looked up.

'He has very little memory of what happened after he was out.'

'Anyway, you didn't write that bit about coming straight home on your little piece of paper here,' I said, waving it in his face.

He grabbed the paper from me, pulled a pen from his shirt pocket, and squeezed in another sentence.

As soon as I have seen Dean Jones in hospital, we can leave.

'No.' As soon as I said it I knew I didn't really mean it. I think Rahul did too.

'What did you say?' he asked, flabbergasted.

'Oh, well, okay,' I said, shaking my head. I thought for a moment that he was about to hug me. Instead he stuck out his hand. I took it.

'You won't regret this. I promise.'

We decided that I would stay the night at Rahul's

on Sunday. Dad would drive me over to his place late in the afternoon. We would say that we wanted to put in a good couple of hours on our cricket projects as Mr Pasquali would be checking on our progress on Monday morning. We felt sure there wouldn't be a problem.

'You're lucky, Rahul. I found some old *Wisdens* in Dad's garage last weekend. I'm pretty sure he had the 1988 one.'

'Fantastic. You won't forget it, will you?'

'I'll try not to.'

Monday — afternoon

Nat had set the hallway up for a monster game of indoor cricket. She had bundled together 25 pairs of socks, all different shapes, sizes and colours. The game was simple, but heaps of fun. She would throw the socks at me as hard as she could. The wicket was an open door behind me. I had to belt the socks with the bat. The scoring was simple.

○ *Side wall*	*1 run*
○ *Side wall on the full*	*2 runs*
○ *Back wall*	*4 runs*
○ *Back wall on the full*	*6 runs*
○ *Caught out by Nat, or bowled*	*lose 10 runs*

Having 25 pairs of socks was great — 25 deliveries. It meant she had raided all available drawers in the house and that I was a good chance to make my 50 —

as long as Mum didn't catch us first. If I got my 50 I would definitely be giving Nat a bat.

'Nat, you want a hit?' I asked her. I'd made 67, but had been bowled once and caught once. I was happy with 47.

'Only if you bowl under-arm.'

'No probs.' We gathered up the socks and I thought of Ally, the catcher in softball, as I pinged the socks at Nat, who was swinging the bat like a softballer.

After dinner I put through a call to Ivo at the hospital. He sounded pretty flat.

'How are you feeling, Ivo?'

'I've been better. But Mum says I'm over the worst.'

'So will you be in there long?'

'Probably another couple of days. I got some internal bleeding which they want to monitor, or something. They had to operate, too.'

I didn't want to ask about the actual crash. I was assuming that no one else was hurt.

'Watch out for driveways, Toby.' Ivo's voice was quiet.

'You were on your bike?'

'Yup. Remember that day in the gym when I had that headache?'

I nodded.

'I was riding home and could hardly see, my headache was so bad, then this car rammed into me.'

'Geez. They probably weren't even looking.'

'I think we both weren't.' There was a pause.

'The cricket's going well. We've got a one-dayer coming up this weekend.'

'Oh, cool. They're the best, aren't they? When you can go home with a result. Hang on.' I heard Ivo talking to someone. 'I'd better go, Toby. Thanks for ringing.'

I liked Ivo. And I felt sorry for him, stuck in a hospital bed. Still, it sounded as if it wouldn't be too long before he was back with us playing cricket. I wondered if Ally would be willing to give up her wicket keeping to him.

I rang the hospital again and this time asked for Jim, but he wasn't available to talk.

'Is he okay?' I asked.

'Who's calling?' said a bossy voice.

'His grandson,' I lied.

'Well, you ask your mum or dad to ring.'

Maybe it was time to try a new one. A new fib, that is.

Wednesday — afternoon

We had our library session on Wednesday. Rahul told us all, including Mr Pasquali, more about his interviews. The one with Dean Jones had been by phone. Even Scott Craven was listening, though he pretended to be working. Gavin Bourke was so interested that he started asking a question — before Scott gave him a not-so-gentle whack in the ribs.

119

'Go on, Gavin. That sounded like a good question,' said Mr Pasquali, giving Scott a bit of a warning look.

'Well, he said that you'd actually have to be there to get a feel for the heat.' Rahul was looking at me, pointedly. 'He said it was just shocking. And smelly, too. There must have been some sort of sewerage place, nearby.' Everyone was saying 'yuk' and 'gross' and wrinkling their noses.

'It was gross!' I said, without thinking. 'I mean, it would have been,' I stammered. 'Rahul was telling me about it earlier.' I felt my face going red.

I had brought Dad's copy of the 1988 *Wisden* to school. At the end of the library session I ducked over to the photocopier and copied the page describing the tied Test match. The scorecard for the game was on the second page.

I didn't know what to expect when the sheets came out, but I was relieved to find that I could read them without a problem. The writing and numbers were clear and still. It must be the *Wisden* book itself that was the trigger for the time travel.

I folded the pages and put them in my pocket. I would practise with those, training my eyes to go straight to the correct spot. Hadn't Jim said that, with practice, you could go to any specific part of a game by looking at the relevant section of the scorecard?

Rahul's interview with Mr Bright, as he called him, was great, too.

'Poor Ray Bright,' said Rahul. 'You know, he was very, very sick too, just like Dean Jones. He almost didn't play. He was so relieved when Australia won the toss and batted. It meant he didn't have to go out into the field.'

'So he just watched from the comfort of the dressing room?' I asked.

'Comfort? Oh no. He lay on a table all day with wet towels on him. He doesn't remember anything about that first day until the captain, Allan Border, came up to him with about half an hour to go and said, "You're night watchy."'

'Night what?' someone asked. Everyone was leaning forward, listening to Rahul.

'Night watchy. Night watchman. You come out if a wicket falls close to the end of play to protect the batters up the order.'

'Sounds stupid to me,' said Scott.

Rahul looked at him. 'Well that's what they did. And sure enough, a wicket fell and poor Ray Bright had to struggle off his sick bed — having eaten nothing all day — and walk out into 40°C heat to face the Indian bowlers.'

There was a pause.

'Well?' I asked.

'It will all be revealed in my talk,' Rahul said, smiling.

'Yeah but what happened to Bright?' Gavin asked.

'You'll hear it all when I present my assignment,' said Rahul with a cheeky grin. There were a few groans of disappointment. 'It'll be just as if I was really there,' he added.

I gave him a look. He just shrugged and smiled.

In a 1903 game between Victoria and Queensland, Victoria used only two bowlers in each innings. In the first, Saunders 6/57 and Collins 4/55 took all the Queensland wickets. In the second, two different bowlers grabbed all 10 wickets (Armstrong 4/13 and Laver 6/17).

15 **The Proof**

Thursday — morning

BEFORE school started the next day, Jimbo approached me when I was talking to Ally, Jay and Georgie.

'Hey, Jimbo,' I said.

'Toby, can I ask you something?'

I moved away from the others and Jimbo followed.

'I've been thinking a bit about our chat the other day. I want to find out some more about what happened the day my father decided to walk away from cricket, and I thought you might be able to help me.'

'Oh,' I was a bit shocked. Jimbo was the sort of guy who never asked for anything. 'How could I do that?' I asked.

'All I know is that it happened on his birthday, which is the same day as the Boxing Day Test match. And I've also been hearing some pretty amazing things about some *Wisden* books and your ability to time travel from a library.'

'You have?' I asked, surprised.

'Yes, from Rahul, and he isn't the sort of guy to make up stuff like that.'

'Rahul told you?' I was stunned.

'Not as such. But like I said, I've heard things. You know how you do.'

I wasn't exactly sure what he meant, but somehow, if there was anyone who would know what was going on without appearing to — or even seeming interested — it was probably Jimbo.

'Anyway, I rang up my grandfather and found out that Dad's game wasn't far from the MCG itself. It was in a big park where there are heaps of ovals and grounds.'

'Hmm. So we go back to the Test match, then try and get to the ground where your dad is playing. And then what?' Two lines from the poem ran through my mind.

> Don't meddle, don't talk, nor interfere
> With the lives of people you venture near.

'Nothing. I just want to see and understand for myself why my father has made this decision. Then maybe I can accept it and we can get on better.'

I thought of Rahul and his reaction to the Madras Test.

'Jimbo, strange things happen when you travel through time. You sort of lose control. You might do something stupid. If you interfere with the past it can change things and stuff up the present.'

Jimbo looked at me hard. 'I can be trusted, Toby.'

Jimbo rang his mum during lunchtime. He'd said she was a safer bet for getting permission for him to come round to my place.

'Yeah?' I asked as he put the phone down.

He nodded.

'Yeah. I think she was actually pretty pleased. Dad's going to pick me up at nine o'clock. He's working late. I think that helped. Should you ring up your parents?'

'Nah, it'll be fine. I'm always bringing home friends. They're used to it.'

I introduced Jimbo to Mum and Nat after school when they collected me. Mum seemed pleased that I was bringing home a new friend. She celebrated by stopping off for ice creams on the way home.

Nat had taken a fancy to Jimbo right from the outset, and I had to wait till she had given him the full tour of the house before we could get upstairs and onto the computer.

'Can we do corridor cricket?' Nat whispered to me at my bedroom door. 'I'm gonna get every pair of socks in the house — you'll see.'

'Okay, Nat, but later, okay?'

We logged into the best site on cricket that I knew. I had it bookmarked and often went there myself to check up on various games, especially the ones that Dad spoke about.

Every game — Test match, World Cup, one-day international and any other official first-class game — was listed. Most of them had full scorecards and match reports and some of the later ones even had a commentary so you could read what happened, ball by ball.

'Jimbo, what year did your grandpa say for that game with your dad?'

'Not sure, but it was early '80s and the Boxing Day Test was an Ashes one, which means —'

'Yep. Australia–England,' I said, excitedly. I scrolled down, searching for the December Tests played in Australia. I knew that 1982 was an Ashes series; since England only came out every four years, it would have to be that year.

'Oh my God, Jimbo.'

'What?'

'It's the 1982 Boxing Test match. The one that Border and Thomson had their huge last-wicket partnership and nearly won the game for Australia. Better still, Dad's got the *Wisden* down there in the garage.'

'What do you mean?'

'The *Wisden*. It's what we need to get there. And the exact game is down there, in the 1984 *Wisden*!'

We spent the next 10 minutes looking over the scorecard. I told Jimbo the story about the match that I still loved having Dad tell me.

I was just up to the final morning when Dad called us down for dinner.

'No worries. I'll get him to finish the story. He won't mind.'

We raced downstairs and into the kitchen. Dad told the story during dinner. He went a bit overboard when he got to the part about everyone stopping what they were doing to listen and watch the game. This time he had parliament stopping and trains and buses coming to a complete standstill as the whole country tuned into those fateful last minutes.

After dinner — and a quick game of corridor cricket — we raced back upstairs.

'Okay, here's the plan. We're going to head out to play some cricket in the nets. On the way we grab the street directory from the car —'

'And the *Wisden* book from the garage?' Jimbo added.

'And the *Wisden* book from the garage. No! We'll go to the garage. Let's go from there.'

Jimbo nodded excitedly. In fact, it was the most excited I'd ever seen him.

'You are so going to like this,' I told him.

'It'll be the best nets session I've ever had!'

I gathered up some loose change from my desk and we headed out, saying we were going for a hit in the nets at the oval across the road.

'You expecting that someone has left all the gear there for you, too?' Dad asked as we headed out the front door.

But Jimbo was a quick thinker. 'I left my kit down in your garage, Mr Jones, we're going to take that.'

'Fair enough. You want an extra bowler?'

We stood there shuffling our feet.

'Then again, maybe I'll clean up the kitchen first.'

'Okay, Dad.' I felt a bit bad. Dad loved a hit. I'd make it up to him. We'd have a massive hit over the weekend.

A few minutes later the two of us were standing in the garage. Jimbo was holding the street directory, and I was holding the *Wisden*.

'Here Jimbo. You find the Boxing Day Test match. Check the contents page.' I passed him the *Wisden* and took the directory from him. I found the MCG and looked around for some green patches — ovals where his dad might have played.

'Did your grandfather have a name for these ovals, Jimbo?'

'Not that I recall. He just said that there were stacks of ovals, for rugby and hockey and soccer. Footy, and of course, cricket. Oh, and they were next to a hospital. A hospital that had — probably still has — a helicopter service. You know, for emergencies.'

'Yep, I know.' Jimbo heard the excitement in my voice. 'I know exactly, I think.'

I flicked to the next page.

'Got it. I reckon we'll just take this with us,' I said to Jimbo, holding the open page to him.

'Here we go, England in Australia and New Zealand. Page 879.' Jimbo flicked through the book.

'Toby, you can get to any of these games? And this is just one *Wisden*!'

'Yep. I think so. As long as there's a scorecard for me to look at.'

Jimbo was shaking his head.

'This is just crazy.' He was searching for the right page. 'What Test match was it?'

'The fourth.'

'Here we go. Pages 898 and 899. This is it.'

'Okay, let's swap again.' We passed the books back.

'What happens to the *Wisden*? Does it come with us?'

'No, it sort of just falls to the ground.' For the first time, Jimbo began to look a bit nervous.

'You okay?'

'Yep — let's do it.'

'Here, grab my hand.' Jimbo took it. We sat down on the floor of the garage, next to the open kit.

I looked at the page of the *Wisden*. I must have been getting better at it, because almost straight away the shifting swirl of names and numbers had settled. Soon I saw a Cook, then a Fowler.

'Cook, Cook,' I said, slowly and clearly.

'Now, Jimbo,' I whispered as the familiar sound of rushing air and pressure surged through me.

A second later we were standing outside the MCG. I'm not quite sure how we managed to be outside the ground, but it was a good place to be. I had focused hard on the names of the first few English players on the *Wisden* page, and as I sensed the movement, kept my eyes away from the numbers. Even then, we had no idea how long it would take to get to the ground and then how long before whatever happened to Jimbo's father actually happened.

Jimbo looked totally stunned.

'Don't ask,' I said. 'Just trust me. It works. We've just got to blend in.' I looked at him. He was wearing runners that looked three sizes too big, the laces were undone, his cap was on back to front and his shorts went down below his knees.

'Blend in as best we can,' I added, spinning my cap the correct way. Jimbo's mouth hadn't closed.

We must have been the only two people walking away from the game. It was a beautiful sunny day and hordes of people with cheerful faces and huge Eskies were streaming towards the ground. Tight T-shirts, tight shorts, small white towelling hats, moustaches and thongs were everywhere. I felt as if I was from another planet, especially as I was walking away from the start of a Boxing Day Test match.

I spotted a line of taxis dropping people off.

'C'mon, Jimbo.'

'Yep. Just don't leave my sight, Toby. You hear?'

'I won't.'

It proved easier than we thought and we didn't

130

need the directory. We climbed into the back seat of a taxi, gave the driver the name of the park and took off.

The cab driver's radio was blaring out a song I'd heard on one of those radio stations that play 'Golden Oldies' music.

'I know this song,' I said to the driver.

'"Eye of the Tiger"? Of course you do — it's on the radio all the time.' He smiled.

I reached into my pocket and pulled out some coins.

'Seven dollars will do you,' said the driver. I handed over the coins. The driver grunted.

'Well you can keep your foreign coin. That's no good to me.' He tossed a two-dollar coin back.

I opened my mouth, then closed it again quickly. He passed me back a few more coins.

We jumped out of the taxi and headed across the grass towards the first of the cricket games being played.

'Hope none of those coins you have were made in the 1990s,' Jimbo whispered to me. I hadn't thought of checking. But it was unlikely the taxi driver would check himself. Still, it was a mistake. To have a coin floating around for 10 years before it had actually been made was something Jim would not be impressed with.

Jimbo had recovered well during the car trip, pointing out a few landmarks on the way that hadn't changed. I think he was trying to convince himself that he wasn't actually 20 years back in time.

There were a number of games going on, but it didn't take us long to find the correct game just by asking for Jimbo's father's team. I could sense that Jimbo was getting nervous, what with the time travel and now the thought of seeing his father. He had been pretty calm during the travelling part, saying little. But now he was edgy.

'Remember, don't get involved,' I warned him. 'We're just here to watch, from the outside.'

Jimbo licked his lips, and nodded. 'Yep. I know.'

We sat down by a tree and watched the game. A few wickets fell but nothing much seemed to be happening.

'I reckon that's him coming in to bat now,' Jimbo said, as we watched a guy wearing glasses stride out to the pitch.

The first ball was a lifter and Jimbo's dad just managed to fend it off his chest. The fielders were urging on the fast bowler, who we hadn't seen bowl before.

'C'mon, Cravo, give it to him!' a fieldsman yelled.

'Oh my God,' I whispered. 'It's Scott Craven's dad!'

I stared at the bowler. He was big and strong, mean and fast, just like his son was going to be.

'Like father, like son,' I whispered.

But Jimbo wasn't listening. The next delivery reared up and struck Jimbo's dad a glancing blow on the side of the head. The next ball thudded into his chest. Jimbo winced and jumped to his feet.

'Hey!' he shouted. 'He's a tail-ender.'

A few of the fielders turned to look. Scott's dad, who was bowling, didn't. I grabbed Jimbo by the arm and pulled him down.

'Jimbo, no!' I said to him. 'You can't interfere. Remember?'

The last ball of the over was another bouncer and it caught Jimbo's dad right above the eye. Jimbo gasped as his dad crumpled to the ground. His bat fell from his hand and toppled against the stumps. There was a shout of 'Howzat?' from the bowler. The umpire nodded, then raised his finger.

'Yeah!' shouted Craven and he pumped his fists in the air just the way I'd seen Scott do it so many times before.

I looked at Jimbo. There were tears streaming down his face and his fists were clenched. He wasn't moving, though, which must have taken a lot of self-control.

A few of the fielders had run in to help Jimbo's dad. There was blood streaming down his face. For a moment I felt sick, not only because of the injury, but because of the rule that allowed a bowler to intimidate a player in that way, and even get him out just because he had lost control of the bat after being smacked in the face.

It just didn't seem fair and I could sort of understand Jimbo's dad's decision never to play again.

The highest score made on debut (someone's first match) in women's cricket was by Michelle Goszko. She scored 204 in the first Test against England in 2001. She was playing for Australia.

16 The Enemy

'C'MON, Jimbo. We've seen enough. Your dad'll pull through. Otherwise you wouldn't be here, watching this.'

He wiped the tears from his face.

'Jimbo, wait here. I'm just going to check the scorecard, and make sure it was Craven. Okay?'

He nodded and watched forlornly as his father was helped from the field. I raced over to a group of players, standing and waiting for their batters to arrive. The fielding team had headed off in a different direction.

I wondered whether it mattered if Jimbo's dad actually saw me. Would he remember my face? Would anyone else? Surely not. But I certainly wouldn't be doing anything stupid or freaky that someone might remember. Just in case.

'Can you hear me?'

I froze.

A harsh, gravelly voice had whispered in my ear. I spun around.

A tall man wearing a hooded cloak was walking

away from me. Had he been talking to me? Everyone else was looking at Jimbo's dad, who was sitting on a chair, with ice and a blood-soaked towel wrapped around his face.

I turned away quickly. No one else seemed to have noticed him. And yet how could they miss him? When I turned back again he had disappeared.

I raced over to Jimbo. My heart was thumping.

'Jimbo!' I yelled. He turned.

Then suddenly there was the creepy man again — between the two of us. Again he seemed to have come from nowhere. He had his back to me and was walking towards Jimbo. He looked so out of place in the park here, but still no one saw him. The few people scattered around the ground kept on with their picnics or their walking. The man was tall, but the weird cloak he was wearing made him look bigger than he was. He definitely looked sinister. He kept his head down and his back to me.

I stopped. Jimbo wasn't moving either. He raised his eyebrows slightly, as though he was asking me if everything was okay.

No, Jimbo! Everything's not okay! I tried to will my thoughts across the space between us.

'What do you want?' I asked the man, my lips trembling.

'You're going to help me, you hear?' he said, but without turning his head. His voice hissed and spat. He was only a few metres away. A horrible stench came from him.

135

'Y-y-yes,' I stammered.

The figure stopped and turned slowly.

I seized my moment. I yelled at Jimbo, then started reciting the first line of the poem. I wanted a glimpse at the man's face, but the need to escape was more urgent.

I kept on with the poem, dashing towards Jimbo and grabbing his hand as the final words of the second line came out.

My head crashed into the side of the garage and Jimbo piled on top of me a moment later. He looked at me incredulously as he gathered himself up.

For a moment neither of us spoke. Jimbo was breathing hard and staring at me.

'Jimbo,' I stammered. 'Did you see that man? Who was he?'

'I dunno.'

We both turned at a noise from further back in the garage. Without another thought we scrambled up and out of there. Then we stopped, hearts pumping.

'My kit,' Jimbo said, looking at the garage door swinging to and fro.

'Yep. The directory too. C'mon, let's get it.'

'Then straight back into the house?'

'Yep.'

We snuck in, eyes down, avoiding the darkness near the back, heading for the kit and the directory. I found the *Wisden*, closed it and shoved it back into its box. We were out again within moments.

'Toby?'

I turned and looked at Jimbo.

'I'm sorry —' I began.

'No. Thanks. That was incredible.'

I nodded. 'I know.'

I raced up the path to the front door and nearly crashed into a man standing on the first step. I almost fainted in fright.

'Hello Dad,' I heard Jimbo say.

I looked up. How long had he been watching us for?

'You boys been playing cricket?'

I didn't like the way he said the word playing.

'Actually, we've been watching cricket, Dad,' Jimbo replied.

Well, it was an honest answer.

The front door opened. It was Mum. She was nodding and smiling and welcoming Jimbo's dad into the house. As we followed them in I wondered if things could really change between Jimbo and his dad.

What a shocker. Sometimes, in the early days of cricket, teams got caught on stickies. These were rain-soaked wickets that were drying out. Wickets back then were never covered. On this particular day, Victoria, playing against the MCC, were knocked over for 15. They lost their first four wickets without a run being scored. And it would have been 5/0, but the next guy was dropped.

17 The Advice

Saturday — morning

'SO, you guys went on the prowl instead of to the nets the other night?' Dad said to me first thing on Saturday morning. I'd slept in on Friday morning and Dad had got home too late to catch up with me on Friday night.

'Yeah,' I grinned, trying to look relaxed. I sat down, hoping that I didn't look as tired as I felt.

'Gee, you look whacked,' Mum said to me, one hand on my shoulder, the other setting down a bowl of cereal.

So much for that hope, I thought to myself.

'Big game today,' I explained. 'Kept on going over it. Couldn't get to sleep.'

'Well, if it hadn't been raining for the last six hours, I would have to agree with you, Toby. John Pasquali phoned through about an hour ago. We thought we'd let you sleep on a bit.'

I was in such a daze that I hadn't even noticed the

grey day outside, the water on the window and that cosy feeling when you wake up and it's raining on a non-school day.

'It's going to be this Thursday, after school,' Dad said.

'Which means we'll all be able to watch, honey,' Mum said.

Nat had tennis on Saturday mornings, which kept her and Mum away. Then again, as Mum often pointed out, my cricket kept Dad and me away from Nat's tennis too.

'So, we can all go to tennis this morning,' Mum said.

'Sure,' I replied. I was glad to tag along. It might take my mind off the creepy man Jimbo and I had met the previous night. Nat was a great tennis player, too. She played against girls way older than her — and usually won.

After tennis I asked Mum if I could go and visit Ivo at the hospital.

But when I got there, a nurse told me that he wasn't allowed to have any visitors. I took the lift up one floor, but this time skulked around a bit, making sure I wasn't seen by any of the nurses.

The door to Jim's room was slightly open. I pushed it and walked in. Jim looked pale and weary, lying there alone on the far side of the room.

'Jim, it's me. Toby.'

He smiled but didn't open his eyes.

'Ah, dear boy. So good of you to come. Tell me of your adventures.'

And I did. I told him everything. I told him about India and Dad's *Wisdens* in the garage. I told him how I had taken Jimbo back to see his dad. Jim winced on hearing that, but he didn't look angry. He didn't look strong enough to be angry. And I told him about the man I'd seen.

Suddenly Jim's eyes were open, his body tense.

'Describe him, Toby.'

'He was tall — and looked really weird. He had on a long hooded cape, so I couldn't see his face. I sure could smell him, though!'

Jim sighed, but he looked worried.

'He said something about helping him.'

Jim closed his eyes, and settled back on his pillows.

'You must not carry, Toby. You must not take others with you. You are exposed and vulnerable when others are with you. I'm sure that's how he found you. Do you understand me, Toby?'

'Yes,' I croaked, for a moment almost forgetting to breathe.

'Which means that my one selfish hope of getting back to 1930 may never come to pass.'

'But why don't you just go?' I asked.

'No, Toby. I have respected that warning all this time. And now, I'm too old to travel. Especially those distances. No, I would need someone young, like yourself, to get me there.'

'I'll carry you,' I said.

For a moment, as I looked down at his sad face and tired body, I felt as though there was nothing I wanted more than to get Jim back to see that 1930 game when Don Bradman made his big score.

'Are you okay, Jim?'

He opened his eyes again, and this time turned his head slightly to look at me directly.

'No, Toby. I'm very tired.' He kept on staring at me. He smiled. 'If everyone's life has a limited number of innings, then perhaps I have seen my Don Bradman innings anyway.'

The door of the ward opened. A nurse bustled in. She carried a clipboard.

'Come along,' she said to me.

'I must think more about this man, Toby.' Jim had grabbed my hand and was holding it tightly.

'Off you go now, mister. That's enough chatting. You'll wear poor Jim out,' the nurse said. She pointed to the door.

'Please!' The nurse and I stopped, surprised by the rifle-crack of Jim's voice.

'Please,' he repeated, less sharply. The nurse looked puzzled. She looked at her watch and busied herself with Jim's chart.

'What does he want?' I asked. I still couldn't believe the world I was entering and talking about with Jim.

'That, I don't know, Toby. But I can tell you that —'

'Well, I know what I want,' the nurse interrupted, writing something on a chart. 'Some peace and quiet in here.'

'We will talk again, Toby and I shall tell you more of what I know.' He turned his weary body slightly to face

141

me. 'It's time to go, Toby.'

'It most certainly is,' said the nurse.

I stared at Jim's worn face. His bottom lip was twitching.

'Have you learnt the poem off by heart?' he whispered.

Ignoring the nurse, I remained by the bed and recited the poem for him. I got to the end without missing a line. By then it looked as though Jim had fallen asleep. I turned to go.

But Jim wasn't asleep.

'It's one thing to say the words of the poem. It's another thing altogether to understand and honour them, Toby.'

'I'm doing my best. I could just walk away from it all,' I said.

'You most certainly could.'

I left Jim's room wondering for a moment whether I should just stay in my normal world. My year. My time. Forever.

Three Test players have taken 4 wickets in 5 balls. M.J.C. Allom achieved this in his first-ever Test match for England, against New Zealand in the 1929/1930 season. When another Englishman, Chris Old, managed the feat, in 1978 against Pakistan, he took 2 wickets, then bowled a no ball, then took another 2 wickets. Wasim Akram, for Pakistan, took his 4 wickets against India in the 1990/1991 series.

18 The Return

Sunday — afternoon

DAD dropped me off at Rahul's at five o'clock on Sunday afternoon. Rahul greeted me at his gate looking very excited.

'Look! I've got some rupees, notepaper, a camera —'

'No camera, Rahul. No way,' I told him.

'Oh, well. It was a long shot.' He grinned.

I was so keyed up I didn't eat much at dinner time. Rahul's family were always very polite and pleasant. Rahul had a sister and another brother, both younger than him. They asked me heaps of questions, and made me very much the centre of attention.

When we went to bed Rahul and I chatted quietly for about half an hour after his mum had come up and said goodnight. The rest of the house was quiet.

'Are you sure there's nothing else you're going to do, Rahul?' I asked for the hundredth time.

'No, Toby. I just want to get a quick look at the game, then see Dean Jones in the hospital.'

'Okay. A quick look and then we're back. You hear me?'

'I hear you,' he grinned at me.

'And if we're nowhere near the hospital, then —'

'Then we maybe get a quick look at the game, and come home,' Rahul finished.

'And have you thought about the fact that we might not be anywhere near the hospital, or have no way of getting there?' I asked him.

'Of course. I have worked hard on this.'

I was less confident.

'It's my call, Rahul.'

'It's your call, Toby.'

'Right. Let's do it.'

We walked over to the lamp and I opened the *Wisden* up to the correct page. The words swirled and spun, round and round.

'Rahul,' I whispered. 'Point at the bit about Dean Jones' big innings.'

'Here,' Rahul said, pointing to a spot halfway down. I grabbed his hand, trying to bring to focus the swarming letters.

Rahul was reading the words. All I saw was a swirly mess.

'"On the second day, Jones ..."' Rahul spoke the words that I was trying to decipher. He read on, and the swirl became letters, and the letters became words ...

'Come on, Toby!'

I looked about. The smell and the noise were

like last time. Again, we seemed to have arrived in a quieter spot, behind one of the stands. This time we walked towards the noise — the ground itself.

The crowd was chanting and the noise was huge. It was a constant roar, occasionally rising to a crescendo when something happened out on the field.

The first thing we both did was turn our heads to the scoreboard. Australia was batting. Dean Jones was on 209.

'It's okay, they'll get him soon,' Rahul called out. He was excited with the knowledge he had and that the other 25,000 people at the ground didn't.

'Rahul!' I exploded. 'No!'

'No one is listening,' he said.

I looked back out across the brown oval. The stench in the air was making me cough and gag. Dean Jones looked exhausted. The other batter — that must have been the captain, Allan Border — was talking to him. Dean was looking at the pitch. A moment later he moved away. His body shook as he tried to vomit.

He hit a ball way out into the deep and walked the single. Walked the whole way. But that was the last run he made.

Rahul had moved a few metres away and was talking to someone — another kid. I moved across to him, worrying about what he might be saying.

Just as I got to him there was a tremendous roar from the crowd.

I looked up. Dean Jones had just been bowled. Everyone was jumping up and down, screaming their lungs out.

'Come on,' Rahul shouted to me, 'this is our chance. Let's go.'

He dragged me away, down the way we had come. We walked around behind a big stand where we waited for a few moments.

'How do you know we're in the right spot?' I asked him. 'And what do we do when he comes out? Hop in the ambulance with him and tell them we're doctors?'

'It's okay, Toby. Like I told you, I've been doing research. It's all worked out.'

We waited and waited.

'So maybe he doesn't go to hospital,' I said.

'Don't worry. He'll be having his iced bath —'

'Listen!' I called.

Above the noise of the crowd, away to our right, was the sound of a siren. It was getting closer.

'Dean Jones has just collapsed onto the floor,' said Rahul. 'He is cramping severely. The ambulance will be here in a moment.'

We stepped back as the siren got closer. People were coming from everywhere. It seemed as if we weren't the only ones who knew what was about to happen.

A stretcher was taken from the ambulance and wheeled through a door. A few minutes later the door opened again and a few men appeared. Dean lay on

146

the stretcher. His eyes were open but he looked as if he wasn't really noticing anything. I took another step back. Rahul didn't.

We followed the group, about 10 metres behind them, through a gate and out into a car park, where the ambulance waited. The crowd was getting bigger. Everyone was talking excitedly.

'What now?' I asked, feeling frustrated. 'We steal a car and chase them?'

'No, silly. Come on.'

Rahul seemed to know exactly where he was going. We came to a line of taxis. Rahul leant down to the open window of the first cab and spoke to the driver. A moment later he motioned me to get inside the taxi. If anything, it was hotter inside the car than out.

'What did you say?' I asked.

'Can you take us to the hospital, please?' He smiled. There was something more happening here, I sensed. But I couldn't for the life of me work out what.

'Are you really so interested in seeing Dean Jones lying in a hospital bed?' I asked him.

'Oh yes, terribly,' he replied. Even Rahul was sweating in the heat. 'You see my whole assignment is based around Dean Jones' innings. Did you know that some of the Australian staff wanted him to come off at tea, when he was about 200? Did you know that he walked his last 20 runs? And it was a tie, Toby. The game was a tie!'

'Rahul!' I hissed.

'Oh yeah. Okay.' He was obviously very excited by the whole Dean Jones story. And it looked as if we weren't the only ones who had followed the ambulance in. Cars were parked everywhere, and people were running in all directions, shouting and giving advice. Inside the hospital was no different.

And I had thought the cricket ground was packed! The hospital was swarming. Doctors, nurses, patients, old people, children, visitors — they were everywhere, choking the rooms and corridors.

'Rahul, we'd better stick close.' People were jostling and pushing us from behind.

'Rahul?' I turned right, then left. He had vanished.

'Rahul!' I screamed. But my cry was lost in the noise and bustle.

'Rahul!' Now I was running — pushing and bumping into people. Then I stopped. There was no way I was going to find him like this. I needed to go back to the front and put out a call for him.

'Rahul Prahibar. Please report to the front desk on ground level, immediately,' came the message over the loudspeaker system a few minutes later.

I sat down to wait. It was then that I started to panic. Suddenly the whole idea of sitting here, alone, in a busy hospital in a city in India nearly 20 years ago was too much. I put my head down in my hands, my shoulders starting to shake.

'Not a happy chappy?'

I froze.

148

Slowly I peeled my hands from my face and looked up. A man wearing a white coat, his arms crossed, looked down at me. He was obviously a doctor come to see what was wrong.

At that moment, a screaming, wailing noise erupted from the sliding doors to our left. A woman rushed in, carrying a small child. The piercing noise from the mother drowned out everything else.

Without thinking, I jumped to my feet, charged past the doctor, raced around a corner and was soon swallowed up in the mass of people. I half-walked, was half-pushed into a lift. I didn't care what floor I went to. I got out on the eighth. It was quieter. The noises here were only of crying babies.

I ran over to a nurses' station.

'Please, I'm looking for Dean Jones.' I panted.

The nurse on duty looked at me blankly.

'Emergency?' I asked.

'Ah,' she nodded. 'Ground floor.'

Great. I walked back towards the elevator. The sound of clapping and laughing made me stop. I looked around a corner and down a long corridor.

Rahul was standing halfway down, staring into a large window.

'Rahul!' I screamed in delight, rushing towards him. He didn't move.

'Rahul, come on. We've gotta go. Now!' I stopped. There were tears streaming down his face. He made no noise.

'What is it?' I looked in through the window. A young Indian man was standing by a bed. A lady lay in the bed, a tiny baby in her arms. Other people stood around the bed. The man picked up the baby and kissed it. Everyone clapped and cheered again.

'That's my brother,' Rahul whispered, through sobs.

'Rahul, we shouldn't be here,' I told him. It only needs someone to turn around, and —'

'Toby, I can't remember my brother,' he continued. Behind us the lift clanked and shuddered to a stop. 'I just have to see his face. He's my brother, Toby!'

'Rahul, you've got the rest of your life to see his face. Come on, let's get out of here.'

Finally, Rahul tore his eyes from the scene in front of him.

'My elder brother,' he said. 'The brother who scooped me out of a river of rushing water and threw me into my father's arms. He saved my life. I was just a baby. He was swept away. That's him there. Being kissed and loved.'

A rush of footsteps made me turn. Two men appeared to be bearing down on us. Rahul made a dash for the half-open door, a few metres to his right. I started reciting a line from the poem, reaching out for him as I did so. He shrugged my arm away and reached for the door handle.

'Rahul!' I cried, frightened beyond belief. 'You

can't go in there!' We were lying entangled, at the foot of the door. It started to open wider and we tumbled forward. Grabbing Rahul's ankle I managed to fire off two lines of the poem.

I never turned to see who had been running along the corridor towards us.

We arrived in a heap on Rahul's bedroom floor. A moment later, the door was flung open. Light streamed into the bedroom.

'Rahul! What is it?' Mr Prahibar stood at the entrance. Rahul wiped his face with the back of his hand, struggled up, and fell into his father's arms.

'I think he's had a bad dream,' I said.

'I heard a thump on the floor,' said Mr Prahibar.

'And fell out of bed, too,' I added, lamely.

His dad looked at him kindly.

'What was your dream, son?'

'Dad,' Rahul started sobbing again. 'I dreamt that I w-was at the hospital where my older brother was b-b-born, and you and Mum and all our family were there. And ... you were h-h-holding, w-w-were holding —'

Rahul's dad hushed him, and Rahul fell silent, except for the sobs that were racking his body.

'Rahul and I will go downstairs, Toby. I'm sorry that you've been involved in all this. Come on, Rahul,' Mr Prahibar was saying as they left. 'Let's talk about this dream you had.'

I crawled back into bed. What had I done? Jim was right. The gift of time travel was not meant for others. All sorts of worries and problems swirled round in my head. The light coming through from the partly open door lit up the *Wisden* on the floor. I got out of bed, kicked the door shut then shoved the *Wisden* under the bed. It thudded into the wall.

Nowadays, cricket pitches are covered, cared for, and looked after with great care. But 100 years ago, things were quite different. In a 1910 game between Victoria and South Australia, with a particularly wet wicket, the match was delayed when a frog appeared from a crack in the pitch.

19 The Letter

Monday — morning

AT breakfast the following morning it was as though nothing had happened. Rahul greeted me with a formal handshake. His eyes met mine.

'Thank you, Toby. It was a gift from heaven. I shall not ask you again. Ever. I promise.' He smiled.

'How'd it go with your dad last night?'

'Very good. I sort of knew bits and pieces about what happened, but Dad had never fully explained everything. He said the time would come. I think it was good for him, too. He found it difficult. He was crying too. But it is the best thing to have happened.'

'Does he know about — you know, the time —'

'No. The dream was an excellent idea.'

'It just came into my head,' I said. 'You tell me about it — one day. Okay?'

Rahul looked down at his shoes, then back to me. 'Yes. I will. But not yet. And we'll take Dean Jones' word for it that he went to hospital, eh, Toby?'

153

After school I headed up to my room. I flicked on my desk light, hit 'play' on the CD player and started thinking.

I'd had an idea ticking over in my head. If I could somehow convince Jimbo's dad to change his mind about not letting Jimbo play cricket, then maybe I could get Jimbo onto the team. Surely Jimbo'd want that. But how would I do it? How can you change someone's mind?

I lay on the bed staring at my cricket posters, thinking about Jimbo and his dad. My mind wandered to his house. The hall ...

Then suddenly it came to me. I shot up off the bed, my heart racing. The hall! The cricket kit! The kit that Mr Temple was putting in the garage sale. If I could get back to the game when Mr Temple was hit, and sneak a letter into his kit — a letter that would convince him to change his mind about his attitude to cricket — then maybe, just maybe, he wouldn't notice the letter for all those years that he didn't play cricket. Until, one day ...

I shoved things off my desk and grabbed a piece of paper. I would have to type it. But I'd write a draft first.

Fifteen minutes later I had written a rough copy. I put it aside and headed downstairs for a snack. On the way a thought struck. What if the cricket kit had already been sold? Weren't garage sales usually on a

Saturday morning? I hoped it was next weekend. I already had a plan to get Jimbo's dad looking in the kit.

Monday — evening

This time I would be travelling alone. I was going to head back to the same park that Jimbo and I had visited. With any luck the creepy guy in the long cloak with the scary voice and the nasty smell wouldn't be there. Jim had said that solo travel was safer.

I told Dad I was going to do a bit more cleaning up in the garage.

'And don't come in until I tell you, Dad. I want it to be a surprise.'

'Sounds good to me,' he called from the kitchen. 'You've got as long as you like!'

I managed to arrive a lot earlier this time, and walked to the park. I kept out of the way too, shielded by a clump of trees on the far side of the oval.

I waited patiently. Life here felt gentle. There were birds and dogs and empty spaces. The picnic rugs were out, and people were pouring drinks and opening up containers of sandwiches. As I sat there, enjoying the peace, it occurred to me that there was cricket happening all around the world, and every game, every situation, was different.

As the moment drew near, I started to focus more on the game. I looked at the envelope. I took out the sheet of paper and read it one more time.

You made a decision. And given what happened
to you, it was perfectly understandable. But now
it is time to give someone you love the
opportunity to play the game he loves. And
display the skills that, being your son, he surely
must possess.

I folded the sheet back into the envelope and sealed
it. I made my way down to where the players were
mingling. Some had left. I hunted around for the
cricket bag with the initials R.T. on it. It was right in
among the players, who were moving around.

> *Don't meddle, talk, nor interfere*
> *With the lives of those you venture near.*

I stopped in my tracks. The words had suddenly come
into my head. I looked about, half-expecting someone
close by to be telling me the poem. But no one was
paying any attention to me. As quickly as the words
had come, they were gone.

Without another thought I moved over to the bag. I
bent down. A Gray Nicholls bat lay across the top of it.

'You looking for something?' A voice called
behind me. I turned. One of the players had noticed
me down near the kit.

'Um, no. I saw this fall out when the bat was
thrown onto the kit,' I said, showing him the
envelope. 'I was just going to put it back.' He stared at
me then shrugged.

'Hang on. I'll grab Richard's stuff and you can pack it all in properly.'

He came back a moment later with pads, gloves, a thigh pad, protector and a cap. There was blood on it.

'Good man,' he said. Carefully, I placed the gear into the bag. I slipped the letter down, resting it between the bat and the side of the bag.

I did up the straps.

It could be opened that night. Or maybe, not for years. I got up and walked away, not looking back. When I had reached a tree about 20 metres away, I turned. No one seemed to be paying any attention to the kitbag, or to me.

> *But for every word that boasts ahead*
> *Means lives unhinged, broken, dead.*

Only three batters have recorded over 10,000 Test runs in their careers. Allan Border (Australia) leads on 11,174, followed by Steve Waugh (Australia) who, after the Test series against England in the 2002/2003 season, had scored 10,521 Test runs, and Sunil Gavaskar (India) on 10,122.

20 The *Wisden*

Wednesday — afternoon

I knew Mr Pasquali collected old cricket stuff, so I gave him a call and told him I'd seen a complete cricket kit including a Gray Nicholls bat, maybe 25 years old. I gave him Jimbo's address and told him to check it out.

After that I made the decision — no more time travelling. I would go and see Jim in hospital and tell him it was over. I had tried a few times to get through on the phone. Then finally, on the Wednesday, they told me that he had gone.

'What do you mean — gone?' I asked.

'Who am I speaking to?' the lady at the hospital asked.

I covered the mouthpiece, and tried to explain to Dad as quickly as I could what was going on. Dad took the phone.

'I'm a friend of Jim's, and we're wondering how he is, that's all.'

Dad listened for a moment, said a few 'I sees', then hung up.

'Strange,' he said. 'They're not exactly certain what's happened. Seems he's just taken himself off. Evidently he's done this once or twice before. They're working on it.'

I must have been looking worried.

'Hey, Toby, I know how you feel, but it's not really our problem.'

'Dad, if it's not our problem, and if it's not anyone else's problem, then there's an old sick man alone somewhere, maybe in trouble.'

'Hmm. So what would you have us do?'

'I want to just check out one thing.' I hit redial and passed Dad the phone. 'Ask them if there's a fat book lying open next to his bed. A *Wisden Cricketers' Almanack*.'

'What? You do it!' Dad said, thrusting the phone back at me. 'I'm not going to ring just to ask a question like that.'

I asked for Jim's room number. A few moments later the same sharp voice came on the line. I shoved the phone back at Dad. At least she would listen to him.

'Hello, Peter Jones here. We spoke before. Um, look, it might seem a silly question really, but I was just wondering whether, ah, there was a book, a fat book, next to Jim's bed?'

'Open!' I said, loudly.

'An open, fat book,' Dad added, giving me a pained look. He made a face at me. I smiled, giving him a little punch on the shoulder.

'There is? Really? Right, well, thank you —'

I grabbed the phone. 'Excuse me. This is really important. Please,' I begged. 'Can you tell me the year of the book and the page number that it's open to? Please! Maybe there was a bookmark —'

The phone clicked.

I love my dad so much — 20 minutes later we were striding through the entrance to the Simpson Hospital. We raced up the stairs to Jim's room.

'We've just come to collect that book. It's important to Mr Oldfield,' Dad added.

'Suit yourself. You can take his bag of belongings too. I put the book back on the bedside table,' she added.

Both beds had been made, and the room was empty.

'1931,' I whispered.

'What's that?' Dad asked.

'Maybe we could check the library at the MCG. Jim could be there.'

'Okay, but if he's not there, we'd better let someone else do the searching.'

'Like the police?'

He nodded. 'Like the police.'

* * *

While we were in the hospital we paid a quick visit to Martian, too. He'd been given the all clear and was coming out of hospital the next day.

'When will you be able to play cricket again?' I asked.

He looked across at his dad, who was sitting on the bed next to him.

'Not sure. But it won't be too long, I hope,' Ivo replied.

'That's great,' I said.

We didn't talk much about the accident, but I told him more about the team and how everyone had been going. He was interested in knowing all the scores and stats.

The floorboards creaked and the musty smell of old books hit me as I entered the library, a few paces ahead of Dad. Jim was sitting at the oval table, a glass of water and a plate of sandwiches in front of him.

'Jim!' I cried, rushing over to him. A few heads looked up.

'My dear boy,' Jim looked pleased to see me. Dad stood behind.

'Hello, Jim,' he said.

'Peter, a pleasure. Excuse me for not standing.'

'We've, um, brought your things from the hospital,' I said, putting the *Wisden* and a bag on the table.

'Thank you. My thanks to the pair of you.' Dad was eyeing the *Wisdens* in the bookshelf. 'Do have a look, Peter. The bookcase is open.'

'Did you get there?' I whispered to Jim.

He looked down at the old *Wisden* in front of him and shook his head. 'I tried, Toby, I tried. But instead, I got back here. The place of my last departure. Which was some time ago now. Still, it's good to be back.'

'Are you okay?' I asked.

'Better for being back here, Toby,' he replied. 'What have you got there?' he asked me. I had reached into my pocket and was fiddling with a dice.

Dad turned round. 'Watch out, Jim,' he said, seeing the dice. 'He's going to nab you for a game of dice cricket!'

'Splendid. I shall send for more sandwiches. Come along, let's clear the table here. I'll choose a team from the 1930s.' Jim started to reel off a list of names.

We ended up spending the rest of the afternoon eating sandwiches and playing the best game of dice cricket. Dad was the roller. Jim insisted on giving Don Bradman seven chances because he was so far ahead of everyone else. I managed to make sure Adam Gilchrist and Ricky Ponting got plenty, too. During the game, Jim would suddenly start talking about a player from his team. His memory was amazing. He told his stories as if he'd just returned from the game. A couple of times I noticed Dad looking at me.

'Great stories,' I whispered to Dad at one stage, when Jim had gone off to find a book to check a score.

He nodded. 'Amazing. You two seem to get on very well,' he added.

'Yeah.'

'Something bothering you, Toby?'

'He's very old, Dad,' I said.

'Well, we all have a journey to make. Some are longer than others. I think Jim has had a pretty decent one, don't you?'

'I guess.'

Jim came back, a book in his hand, his eyes shining.

And even though Ricky Ponting scored 143, it wasn't enough to trouble Jim's 'Invincibles'.

I must have been looking a bit down about the result. Dad said to me, 'Head up, Toby.'

I smiled a secret smile.

Then we said goodbye. I think Jim knew that my goodbye was sort of final. When Dad was putting away the *Wisdens* he had pulled out, I leant over and told Jim that I didn't think I would be time travelling again.

He nodded his head, and said nothing.

'Jim, *will* I time travel again?' I whispered, not really wanting to hear an answer.

'Perhaps only to help an old man fulfil a lifelong dream,' he said quietly.

I didn't say anything.

'Come along, Toby.' Dad's hand rested on my shoulder. We shook hands with Jim.

'Toby, I want you to have this,' Jim said, handing me the 1931 *Wisden*.

'Jim, no —' Dad interrupted.

'Please, Peter. Toby deserves this. Please.' Jim's voice was insistent.

I didn't know what to say. I held the precious book in my hands.

'Off you go,' Jim said.

'Well, I hope we catch up again, Jim, and thank you very much for that generous gift. He'll look after it, I promise,' Dad said, shaking Jim's hand.

'Yes, I know he will,' Jim smiled.

I was quiet for a while on the way home.

Dad picked up on my thoughts, as always, and said, 'You okay, son?'

'Dad, I don't have a grandfather, do I?'

Dad flicked his head round, then turned back to the road. 'No.'

'I sort of feel like I do, now.'

'Jim's someone else's grandfather, Toby.'

'Maybe not in this time,' I mumbled. Luckily, Dad didn't seem to hear. 'I wonder where he lives. I wonder who looks after him?'

'Maybe Jim looks after himself.'

'Dad, he's just come out of hospital. He didn't get any visitors.'

'We don't know that, Toby. You can't just enter someone's life and assume he needs your help and guidance.'

We didn't speak for a while until Dad said, 'We'll invite Jim over for a barbecue. How's that?'

'That'd be great, Dad. I reckon he'd love it.'

We were silent once more. I started thinking about my decision to give up time travel. Had I made the right choice? Then I remembered the evil hooded man again, and became convinced that I had.

In 1915, J.C. Sharp, a schoolboy batting for Melbourne Grammar, scored an amazing 506 not out against Geelong College. A team-mate, R.W. Herring, scored 238. The total score was 961 and the game was won by an innings and 647 runs.

21 The Game

Thursday — afternoon

I still couldn't get the thought of the mystery man out of my head as we drove to the ground after school the next day. I had dreamt of him again the previous night. I couldn't work out why he'd been after me. *Was* he after me? Maybe I'd just happened to be in the wrong place at the wrong time.

Still, I didn't have to worry about it any more. And right now, there was a game of cricket to be played. Maybe my nerves were because of the game, and not the time travel stuff.

After all, it was the Scorpions we were up against. I thought we were going to be able to handle the other four teams — Motherwell, TCC, Benchley Park and St Mary's. But the Scorpions were an unknown.

Jono won the toss and decided to bat. Mr Pasquali told us that we were totally on our own today. We would be responsible for the batting and bowling order, the fielding positions and all other decisions. It was a 30-over game, batters retiring at 30 and with a maximum of four overs per bowler.

Of course Scott Craven opened the batting, along with Jono. Five balls and two fours later, Scott was walking back to us, caught behind, for 8. The very next ball, Cameron was bowled. We were 2 for 8.

Rahul had only just managed to get his gear on. Normally he had a routine of tapping the ball up on the edge of his bat to get his eye in. There were some tense moments as Georgie, Jay and I scrambled to get our pads on.

The other opening bowler was even quicker, but maybe not as accurate. His first two balls were wides, but his third smashed into Jono's pads. There was a loud appeal from every player on the ground, and even some of the dads standing in a group away to our left.

The umpire looked hard, then raised his finger.

'Oh, no,' groaned Jay. 'Hey, I'm not ready. Georgie, you go in, can you?'

'Get out there, you wimp!' roared Scott.

'But I can't find my box!' he wailed.

'I'll go,' I said. I gathered up my helmet and gloves, adjusted my thigh pad, and strode out to the wicket, trying to look confident. Rahul met me halfway.

'Toby, we've got to stay in until these two fast bowlers have finished their spell. Don't worry about the runs. Okay?'

That was easy for him to say. He was a regular top-order batter, and he wasn't on strike. I took guard, had a look around the field, then settled over my bat and waited.

A split second later the ball was flying past my head and through to the keeper. I danced on the spot, trying to get some spark into my body. Five minutes ago the openers were walking out to bat and already I was in the firing line. I could see Dad, the newspaper dropped to the ground beside him, leaning forward in his deck chair, concentrating on the game.

I managed to survive the rest of the over, only having to play at one delivery. Rahul scored a single off the first ball of the next over and I was back on strike. I wasn't as nervous now, having played a few deliveries already.

The next ball changed all that. It rose from just short of a length and crashed into the top half of my bat. There was a huge cracking noise as leather struck wood. The ball sailed away over slips and down to the boundary for four. The bat — all except the handle — fell onto the pitch.

There were hoots of laughter from the kids around me. Even the bowler was smiling. A moment later, Craven rushed out, offering me his bat.

'Are you sure?' I asked.

'Course. Just don't snick any or I'll make you lick off the cherry. You hear?'

The bat weighed a tonne. It was all I could do to lift it just as the bowler delivered the ball. But when

I connected, which I did twice more in the over, with a nicer cracking sound, the ball raced away for four.

It's amazing what a few fours can do for your confidence. I swung and missed a few times, and Rahul and I kept on reminding ourselves that it would get easier once the two opening bowlers had finished their spells, but I still managed to find a few gaps, and after 8 overs we had pushed the score along to 3 for 31.

Mr Pasquali was nodding in approval from square leg as we started to pile on the runs. Craven's bat was incredible. Between balls, I let it rest against me, not picking it up until I absolutely had to.

We had got the score to 72 before a guy bowled a quicker, more pitched-up delivery — a yorker. I couldn't jam the bat down quickly enough and the ball slammed into the base of my leg stump. I was out for 29.

I got plenty of cheers and applause as I trudged off.

'Bloody lucky I gave you the bat. You wouldn't have got past 10 without it,' Scott chuckled. He seemed to be in a good frame of mind, considering he'd had two failures in a row with the bat.

'Guess not,' I said. 'Thanks.'

We went on to score 174 with some good hitting from everyone else — including Jason Vo, playing his first game for us. Georgie and Ally belted the bowlers around a bit and made 32 between them.

Our opponents had made the mistake of using up their two best bowlers too early. I wondered if Jono would do the same. I was in for a surprise.

He threw the new ball to me.

'You're up, Toby. Hit the spot.'

I was fired up after my batting. We set an attacking field. My first ball dropped a bit short and in a flash the batter was in behind it, belting it over mid-wicket for four. Jono clapped his hands, yelling encouragement. Craven groaned.

I bowled flatter and faster for the rest of the over but they took 7 off me. Craven bowled a maiden from the other end, the batters not really looking troubled by his pace. Maybe they were used to it, with the practice they got facing their own opening bowlers.

I was on again. Probably for only 1 more over if it went like the first. My first ball was whacked out over mid-on for four. It was a bit of a slog, but it was four. Jono kept the fielders in, though, which was good. I liked it when the batter was having a go.

I sent the next ball (pitched a bit shorter) down much quicker. It fizzed past the bat and Ally took it neatly. One to the bowler. I pitched the third delivery slightly wider outside off-stump. The batter's eyes lit up. He danced out of his crease, took a huge swing, but this time it caught the edge of his bat and Ally completed the catch.

Things settled down after that. I completed my 4 overs, not taking another wicket, but not giving away too many runs either.

Jono kept Craven back for the final overs, and when he came on to bowl his last, they needed 4 runs to win. They had lost 9 wickets. It was a tough field to set. You could sense the tension around the ground. Players, umpires and parents were all on edge.

'It's Madras!' Rahul called to me from mid-off. 'This is exactly the same as Madras: 1 over left, 1 wicket left and 4 runs to get.'

I clapped my hands together, urging everyone on.

I walked in from my position in the covers as Craven charged in to the wicket. It was a good-length ball, a bit slower, and the batter blocked it. He slashed at the next delivery and carved it out to my left. I dived full stretch and got a hand on it. The batters had assumed it would get through. It had 'four' written all over it. I fumbled around, picked up the ball and hurled it to Ally, who had run up to the stumps.

She whipped the bails off. Appeals were screamed from everywhere, even from the other side of the boundary. The umpire stared for a moment at the broken stumps, then shook his head.

Three runs needed for the Scorpions to win the game.

The batter chopped the next ball away between the slip and gully fielders for two more runs. I looked across at Rahul. But it was the two figures behind him that caught my attention. I stared in amazement.

I turned back only when Craven was about to bowl his fourth ball of the over. It thudded into the batter's pads. Craven was on his knees, appealing for lbw. Mr Pasquali shook his head.

'This next one, Scott,' Rahul called across from mid-on.

The scores were level. You could feel the tension. No one was moving. I looked again at the two figures, still and silent, watching from a spot away from the other spectators.

Jono brought everyone in. A single run would win it for them, so we might as well try to prevent that.

It was the second-last delivery of the over. Scott bowled a slower ball. It was bang on target. It caught the batter right back on his crease and smacked into his pads. Craven didn't even appeal. He just kept on running towards the batter, his arms in the air.

The batters were running a leg bye. There were screams and shouts from everywhere.

Finally Rahul, out at mid-off, yelled an appeal. By then, the runners had completed a run, and were scampering away, waving their bats and shouting and cheering. We all raced over to Mr Pasquali. Even Scott had turned around. Mr Pasquali shook his head and headed across to the other umpire. They met at mid-pitch, chatted for a moment, then shook hands and walked off together.

'Looks like everyone's a winner today, Mr Pasquali!' I said to him, picking up the ball. He smiled.

There were two other figures walking away from the ground.

'Jimbo!' I called. He stopped, and turned. His father had an arm around his shoulders. Jimbo nodded a few times, gave me the thumbs up, then turned and walked away.

I turned to Mr Pasquali and said, 'What happened about the cricket kit? Was the bat really a Gray Nicholls?'

'It was, Toby, and the kit was in fantastic condition. But when I went over to check it out, Richard opened up the bag and decided at the last moment to keep it for Jimbo, which I thought was a great idea.'

'That's excellent news!' I exclaimed. I could hardly believe my plan had worked. Maybe time travel could be useful, after all.

'We just need that little extra something in the team to get us over the line,' Mr Pasquali told us a few minutes later. He looked over at a car that was backing away from the oval. 'And I think we might just have the ingredient we're looking for.'

'But who won?' Gavin asked.

'I think Rahul can give us the answer. He seems to know what happened.'

Everyone looked at Rahul.

'It was a tie,' he said. 'Just like the Madras game.'

Monday — afternoon

The moment had finally arrived for the presentations. I couldn't wait to hear what the others had done, as we had all put plenty of effort into our cricket projects.

I sat there listening to all the others, feeling a bit nervous, but enjoying the talks all the same. Mr Pasquali had put me last.

When my moment came. I walked out to the front and opened up the file on the computer that Mr Pasquali had set up.

The first slide appeared on the big screen and I began my talk.

I looked across at the sea of faces in front of me. No one said a word.

'Really, I felt as if I was there,' I said to them.

'Well, it certainly came across that way, Toby. Well done.' Mr Pasquali was nodding and started to clap. The rest of the class joined in enthusiastically.

'Tell me,' asked Mr Pasquali, after the clapping had stopped. 'Where did you get all that detailed information, Toby?'

I bent down and took out a *Wisden* from my bag beneath the table. I held it up to the class.

'Toby!' cried Jimbo, Georgie and Rahul, almost in unison.

Mr Pasquali turned to look at them. 'Is there a problem?' he asked.

'No, no,' they all said at once. Mr Pasquali turned back to me.

'Toby, you were saying?'

'Well, these *Wisden* books, Mr Pasquali, are filled

with all the information you could ever wish for. They have reports on all the games played for the year just passed. They choose the five cricketers of the year. Plus, they have this amazing section where all the records are listed.' I could have kept on going for ages.

'I know. There's always one beside my bed! I'll see if the library can buy some.'

Rahul and Jimbo were staring at me. I looked across at Mr Pasquali. He was jotting down a note in his book. Maybe it was my score for the talk I'd just presented.

'Great,' I said, looking over at Georgie. She smiled.

Mr Pasquali looked up. 'So these *Wisden* books inspired you, Toby?'

Yes, you could say that, I thought to myself as I smiled at him.

BOWLING — THE YORKER

This delivery, sometimes called the 'sandshoe crusher', is a lethal weapon and every fast bowler should use it. Medium-pacers can also use a yorker to good effect.

A yorker is a ball that is pitched up so far that it pitches close to the crease, where the batter is standing.

Its other feature is that it is bowled quicker than the bowler's normal delivery in order to surprise the batter. This combination of speed and fullness can often lead to problems. The batter can be bowled if his or her bat doesn't get down quickly enough, or he or she can be trapped lbw. This happens because the batter doesn't have time to move forward.

It is not an easy ball to bowl. Too much fullness, and you give the batter a full toss to hit. A little too short, and the batter has a half-volley. And these are juicy deliveries for a batter to receive!

There have been 19 tied one-day internationals played since 1984. In only one of these games were the actual scores different. This happened in the 2003 World Cup game when Sri Lanka, chasing South Africa's score of 9/268, got to 6/229 after 45 overs before having to leave the field because of heavy rain. Their innings couldn't be resumed, and the game was declared a tie under the Duckworth-Lewis method.

THE 1999 WORLD CUP

that Toby did his project on

On 9 June, in the 1999 Cricket World Cup, Australia was playing South Africa. An amazing thing happened. Steve Waugh clipped a ball off his pads into the hands of Herschelle Gibbs, fielding in close on the leg side. For a split second Gibbs saw Australia's dream of winning the World Cup lying in the palm of his hand. But as he went to throw the ball into the air to celebrate taking the catch to remove the Australian captain, it fell from his hand to the ground.

Waugh was on 28. About two hours later he hit a ball through mid-wicket to take Australia not only to a memorable win against South Africa but to a semi-final. Steve Waugh ended up scoring 120 not out.

Same teams, but this time it's a semi-final. The winner goes through to play in the final of the 1999 World Cup. Hansie Cronje wins the toss for South Africa and decides to send Australia in to bat.

And it seems a pretty good decision. But after only five balls Australia have lost Mark Waugh for a duck. Ricky Ponting and Adam Gilchrist soon have the situation looking good again, smashing the ball to all parts of the ground.

When the score reaches 54, Ricky chases a wide delivery from Allan Donald and hits it straight to cover. Out! Caught. Then, five balls later, Australia are under the pump again when Allan Donald has Darren Lehmann caught behind for one.

Only 10 runs later, 'Gilly' goes for a big hit outside his off-stump and carves the ball to backward point where Donald takes the catch. Allan Donald has had a hand in the last three wickets to fall. Australia have gone from a steady 1 for 54 to a very shaky 4 for 68.

Michael Bevan and Steve Waugh are proceeding slowly. They can only manage 20 runs between over number 20 and over number 30. South Africa are not taking wickets, but Australia's scoring rate has fallen right back. The pressure is intense. Australia have to be careful as they have only one recognised batsman left.

In the 35th over Lance Klusener is bowling to Waugh. The ball is there to be hit and he launches into a beautiful straight drive for four.

177

To the next ball, he plays another straight drive but lofts it over the boundary rope. Ten runs in two balls. This is more like it ...

Soon the momentum is starting to swing Australia's way. The batting of Steve Waugh and Michael Bevan is productive. But just at the critical moment when they are beginning to get on top, Waugh tries to edge a ball that is too close to his body away through the vacant slips area. All he manages to do is get a thickish edge and present an easy catch for Mark Boucher, the South African keeper.

Michael Bevan and Waugh have taken the score from a worrying 4 for 68 to a more respectable 4 for 158. They have put on 90 runs in just over 23 overs, at a reasonable rate of 3.8 runs per over. But now Australia are 5 for 158. And only three balls later Tom Moody is walking back to the pavilion — out for a duck, lbw to Shaun Pollock. Two wickets have fallen in an over.

Australia still have another 11 overs to face, but the bowlers are going to have to help Michael Bevan, who now needs to bat through the innings if Australia are going to build a reasonable score.

Michael Bevan has played really well. He hardly ever slogs. He knows exactly where there are gaps between fieldsmen and he has the ability to keep the scoreboard ticking along without you really thinking that anything much is happening.

But Australia's bowlers are finding batting difficult against the classy South African bowlers. Warne manages to knock up 18 very handy runs for Australia off only 24 balls. Together, he and Bevan add just under 50 runs in only eight overs. This is a crucial period of the game. Australia only manage to score another six runs after that. Had either lost his wicket earlier, Australia might not have reached 180.

Mark Boucher takes his fourth catch in the 50th and last over of the innings, and Michael Bevan is out for 65. Australia's total is 213 — not a great score. The South Africans feel confident about their chances of winning and going on to the final at Lord's.

But the pitch is wearing, and will suit Shane Warne. Australia have a great bowling attack and a fantastic fielding team. The Aussies will not be giving up until the final ball is bowled, perseverance being a feature of this team.

* * *

The feeling round the ground as the players take lunch is that Australia haven't scored enough runs. The pitch is still a beauty. The clouds of the morning are breaking up and South Africa have bowled Australia out for well inside the 250 runs that many people felt were needed on such a good batting strip. The South Africans will be feeling confident. They have bowled the Australians out inside their 50 overs and have fielded superbly all day. Now it is their turn to bat.

But there is one hope for Australia: the brilliant Shane Warne. The pitch is considered the equivalent of a seventh-day Test wicket. Normally only three or four days are needed to produce a turning Test match pitch, sometimes even fewer.

Shane Warne is about to be let loose on a seven-day-old wicket. Will he be the difference? Or will the accuracy of Glenn McGrath, Damien Fleming and Paul Reiffel do the job for the Aussies?

Time will tell.

The first 12 overs go smoothly for South Africa. The pitch offers nothing for the Aussie 'quicks' and the South African openers are looking comfortable. Gibbs and Kirsten score freely and race the score along to 48. They are not far from taking their side to a quarter of the required total — and, importantly, South Africa have 10 wickets in hand.

Enter Shane Warne. It is the 13th over of the game. His second ball is tossed up, and pitches outside off-stump. Gibbs pushes at it, probably not expecting too much spin. But spin there is. The ball bites back viciously and clips the off-stump.

This delivery, apart from securing a wicket, will almost certainly have sent a few shivers through the South African dressing room. Five runs are added, then Warne is back for his second over. This time he doesn't need a warm-up ball. On his first delivery, again tossed up but this time outside off-stump, Gary Kirsten launches into a big sweep. But the spinning ball finds the edge of his bat and rebounds onto his stumps.

In the space of five balls, Shane Warne has dismissed both openers, and South Africa have stumbled to 2 for 53. Another two balls later it is 3 for 53, with the South African captain, Hansie Cronje, trudging back to the pavilion, caught by Mark Waugh for a duck.

Three wickets have been taken and only five runs added. South Africa need cool heads at the wicket. But Jonty Rhodes and Daryll Cullinan have everyone on edge with their hair-raising running between wickets. No less than three times the Aussies have the chance to run out one of the batsmen. But their throws are off-target.

Shane Warne continues to bowl well and is really troubling Cullinan. Rhodes then attempts another cheeky single — a push straight to Michael Bevan at mid-off. Jonty makes his ground, but he hasn't calculated on Michael Bevan choosing to ping the ball to the batter's end. This time it is a direct hit and Cullinan is run out.

It is 4 for 61 and the Aussies are on top. But now comes South Africa's best partnership of the match. The same partnership for Australia added 90 runs. Jacques Kallis and Jonty Rhodes do almost as well, putting on 84 runs as well as taking the South Africans into the last 10 overs of the game.

But they are still struggling to score quickly. It is going to be a tense finish. South Africa still have six wickets in hand as the 41st over begins.

South Africa have moved to 4 for 144. The game is evenly poised. The South Africans have some big hitters to come, but first, the Rhodes/Kallis partnership needs to be broken. And at last it is, when Michael Bevan takes a catch at deep mid-wicket from a Jonty Rhodes sweep.

Shaun Pollock comes in and knocks up some quick runs. Shane Warne's final over is dramatic. Pollock skies the first ball out to deep mid-off, but Paul Reiffel misjudges the catch. Then Pollock belts Warne for a six and a four. The fourth ball yields a single, and on Warne's fifth delivery, Kallis pushes a catch to captain Steve Waugh.

In the next over, South Africa lose their seventh wicket with the score on 183 when Pollock plays over a yorker from Damien Fleming, losing his middle stump.

South Africa, still 31 runs away from victory, will be confident while Lance Klusener is at the wicket.

The final overs are likely to be dramatic . . .

The pressure is building with every ball. In the 49th over (the second last) Glenn McGrath bowls Boucher with his second ball. But Klusener is hitting cleanly, maybe too cleanly. An easy single off McGrath's fourth delivery becomes an attempted two. But McGrath cleverly pads Reiffel's strong throw onto the stumps — 7 for 196 has become 9 for 198. A single off the last ball means that Klusener has the strike for the last over. Damien Fleming is the bowler.

South Africa need nine runs to win.

Klusener smashes the first ball through the covers for a four.

Five balls left, five runs to win.

Another yorker-length ball, angled in at the batsman, is again clubbed by Klusener — an amazing shot — out through mid-off, for another four.

Four balls left, one run to win. The scores are tied. Steve Waugh brings the fielders in. Fleming changes his angle and comes in over the wicket. Again Lance Klusener belts the ball, but this time it goes straight to a fielder.

At the bowler's end, Allan Donald has backed up a long way. Darren Lehmann picks up the ball and hurls it at the stumps. It misses. Had he hit, the video suggests that Donald would have been run out.

Three balls left, one run to win.

Another whack from Klusener, this time to mid-off. He charges down the wicket for a single. Donald has his back turned, watching the ball. The fielder throws the ball to Fleming at the bowler's end; Fleming then underarms it quickly but safely down to the keeper. By now Allan Donald has set off. But not soon enough. Adam Gilchrist takes off the bails and Donald is run out.

An amazing game finishes in a tie. Australia goes on to the final only because it has defeated South Africa in an earlier stage of the tournament.

In the final, Australia defeats Pakistan comfortably.

1999 WORLD CUP SCORECARD

World Cup Semi-final

17 June 1999, Edgbaston, England
Toss: South Africa • Decision: Send Australia into bat • Result: Tie

Australia Innings	R	B	4s	6s
Adam Gilchrist c Donald b Kallis	20	39	1	1
Mark Waugh c Boucher b Pollock	0	4	0	0
Ricky Ponting c Kirsten b Donald	37	48	3	1
Darren Lehmann c Boucher b Donald	1	4	0	0
Steve Waugh c Boucher b Pollock	56	76	6	1
Michael Bevan c Boucher b Pollock	65	101	6	0
Tom Moody lbw b Pollock	0	3	0	0
Shane Warne c Cronje b Pollock	18	24	1	0

Australia Innings (cont)	R	B	4s	6s
Paul Reiffel b Donald	0	1	0	0
Damien Fleming b Donald	0	2	0	0
Glenn McGrath not out	0	1	0	0
Extras (byes 1 / lb 6 / w 3 / nb 6)	16			
Total (49.2 overs)	**213**			

South Africa Bowling	O	M	R	W
Shaun Pollock	9.2	1	36	5
Steven Elworthy	10	0	59	0
Jacques Kallis	10	2	27	1
Allan Donald	10	1	32	4
Lance Klusener	9	1	50	0
Hansie Cronje	1	0	2	0
	49.2	**5**	**203**	**10**

South Africa Innings	R	B	4s	6s
Gary Kirsten b Warne	18	42	1	0
Herschelle Gibbs b Warne	30	36	6	0
Daryll Cullinan run out (Bevan)	6	30	0	0
Hansie Cronje c M Waugh b Warne	0	2	0	0
Jacques Kallis c S Waugh b Warne	53	92	3	0
Jonty Rhodes c Bevan b Reiffel	43	55	2	1
Shaun Pollock b Fleming	20	14	1	1
Lance Klusener not out	31	16	4	1
Mark Boucher b McGrath	5	10	0	0
Steven Elworthy run out (Reiffel)	1	1	0	0
Allan Donald run out (Fleming)	0	1	0	0
Extras (byes 0 / lb 1 / w 5 / nb 0)	6			
Total (49.4 overs)	**213**			

Australia Bowling	O	M	R	W
Glenn McGrath	10	0	51	1
Damien Fleming	8.4	1	40	1
Paul Reiffel	8	0	28	1
Shane Warne	10	4	29	4
Mark Waugh	8	0	37	0
Tom Moody	5	0	27	0
	49.4	**5**	**212**	**7**

RAHUL'S INTERVIEWS

Part of Rahul's interview with Dean Jones:

RP: Hello Dean.

DJ: Hello, how are you?

RP: Good thanks. What was it like out there during your 210?

DJ: Well it was pretty tough, actually. What made it so hard was the high humidity and the fact that I just couldn't keep any fluid in.

RP: Is it true that you wanted to go off before you were out?

DJ: Oh yes, I was pretty sick during the afternoon. I had got to about 170 and I said to AB (Allan Border) that I'd had enough. He said, 'Righto, we'll get a Queenslander out here. Someone tough who can stand up to it.'

RP: What happened after you were out?

DJ: I don't remember much. I remember being put into a bath filled with iced water and ice. Do you know what? It felt lukewarm! Everything was fine until I decided to get out. My body cramped up completely. Everywhere. I just collapsed in a heap. That's when they decided I needed a visit to the hospital.

RP: Did you get to the hospital?

DJ: Eventually. I'm told it was a pretty hairy ride. We were flying all over the place. The physio with me had to hold me down to stop me from cramping with all the shaking and swerving the ambulance was doing.

RP: What happened when you got to the hospital?

DJ: Well, I'm told that I was taken to casualty. There was a man there who was needing some attention, but when the doctors and other staff realised that a Test cricketer had just arrived, they all left him lying on his bed and raced over to me.

Part of Rahul's interview with Ray Bright:

RP: Ray, some people say you were the hero of the last hour. What happened?

RB: No, there were plenty of heroes out there. I was actually off the field. I was very dehydrated and struggling to stay on my feet.

RP: But you came back onto the field?

RB: Yes. Allan Border, our captain, wanted me to bowl.

RP: What happened?

RB: Well, it was very tense. Lots of shouting and frustration. I managed to get a couple of wickets quickly and that sort of changed the balance of things. India were in a winning position. I think they needed 20-odd runs off the last five overs with four wickets in hand.

RP: And the last over?

RB: The last over. It probably took about 10 minutes. Greg Matthews bowled it. They needed four runs to win. We needed one wicket. Ravi Shastri was batting really well. He was facing. He blocked the first ball and then hit the next for two. He hit the third ball for a single. The scores were tied. The next ball was blocked, but the fifth ball was a wicket!

RP: What was the reaction?

RB: Well, we were jubilant. We were running around very excitedly. Some of us actually thought we'd won. And I suppose, given what the situation was half an hour before, we sort of had.

1986 INDIA v AUSTRALIA SCORECARD

India v Australia Test Match
18–22 September 1986, Madras, India
Toss: Australia • Decision: Australia to bat • Result: Tie

Australia 1st Innings	R	B	4s	6s
David Boon c Kapil Dev b Sharma	122	258	21	0
Geoff Marsh c Kapil Dev b Yadav	22	66	2	0
Dean Jones b Yadav	210	330	27	2
Ray Bright c Shastri b Yadav	30	59	3	1
Allan Border c Gavaskar b Shastri	106	172	14	1
Greg Ritchie run out	13	18	1	1
Greg Matthews c Pandit b Yadav	44	78	5	0
Steve Waugh not out	12	48	0	0
Tim Zoehrer did not bat	0	0	0	0
Craig McDermott did not bat	0	0	0	0
Bruce Reid did not bat	0	0	0	0
Extras (byes 1 / lb 7 / w 1 / nb 6)	15			
Total (170.5 overs) 7 dec	574			

India Bowling	O	M	R	W
Kapil Dev	18	5	52	0
Chetan Sharma	16	1	70	1
Maninder Singh	39	8	135	0
Shivlal Yadav	49.5	9	142	4
Ravi Shastri	47	8	161	1
Kris Srikkanth	1	0	6	0
	170.5	31	566	6

India 1st Innings	R	B	4s	6s
Sunil Gavaskar c & b Matthews	8	21	0	0
Kris Srikkanth c Ritchie b Matthews	53	62	9	1
Mohinder Armanath run out	1	7	0	0
Mohammad Azharuddin c & b Bright	50	64	8	0
Ravi Shastri c Zoehrer b Matthews	62	106	8	1
Chandrakant Pandit c Waugh b Matthews	35	57	4	0
Kapil Dev c Border b Matthews	119	138	21	0
Kiran More c Zoehrer b Waugh	4	21	1	0
Chetan Sharma c Zoehrer b Reid	30	55	2	1
Shivlal Yadav c Border b Bright	19	55	3	0
Maninder Singh not out	0	14	0	0
Extras (byes 1 / lb 1 / w 5 / nb 0)	7			
Total (94.2 overs)	397			

Australia Bowling	O	M	R	W
Craig McDermott	14	2	59	0
Bruce Reid	18	4	93	1
Greg Matthews	28.2	3	103	5
Ray Bright	23	3	88	2
Steve Waugh	11	2	44	1
	94.2	14	387	9

Australia 2nd Innings	R	B	4s	6s
David Boon lbw b Singh	49	92	4	1
Geoff Marsh b Shastri	11	40	0	0
Dean Jones c Azharuddin b Singh	24	39	3	0
Allan Border b Singh	27	41	4	0
Greg Ritchie c Pandit b Shastri	28	29	2	1
Greg Matthews not out	27	25	2	0
Steve Waugh not out	2	7	0	0

Australia 2nd Innings (cont)	R	B	4s	6s
Ray Bright did not bat	0	0	0	0
Tim Zoehrer did not bat	0	0	0	0
Craig McDermott did not bat	0	0	0	0
Bruce Reid did not bat	0	0	0	0
Extras (byes 0 / lb 1 / w 0 / nb 1)	2			
Total (49 overs) 5 dec	**170**			

India Bowling	O	M	R	W
Kapil Dev	1	0	5	0
Chetan Sharma	6	0	19	0
Maninder Singh	19	2	60	3
Shivlal Yadav	9	0	35	0
Ravi Shastri	14	2	50	2
	49	**4**	**169**	**5**

India 2nd Innings	R	B	4s	6s
Sunil Gavaskar c Jones b Bright	90	168	12	1
Kris Srikkanth c Waugh b Matthews	39	49	6	0
Mohinder Armanath c Boon b Matthews	51	113	8	0
Mohammad Azharuddin c Ritchie b Bright	42	77	3	1
Chandrakant Pandit b Matthews	39	37	5	0
Kapil Dev c Bright b Matthews	1	2	0	0
Ravi Shastri not out	48	40	3	2
Chetan Sharma c McDermott b Bright	23	38	3	0
Kiran More lbw b Bright	0	1	0	0
Shivlal Yadav b Bright	8	6	0	1
Maninder Singh lbw b Matthews	0	4	0	0
Extras (byes 1 / lb 3 / w 0 / nb 2)	6			
Total (86.5 overs)	**347**			

Australia Bowling	O	M	R	W
Craig McDermott	5	0	27	0
Bruce Reid	10	2	48	0
Greg Matthews	39.5	7	146	5
Ray Bright	25	3	94	5
Allan Border	3	0	12	0
Steve Waugh	4	1	16	0
	86.5	**13**	**343**	**10**

UNDER-13 SOUTHWESTERN DIVISION

Competition Rules and Draw

There will be six teams competing for the Under-13 Cricket Cup this year.

- Benchley Park
- Motherwell State
- Riverwall Cricket Club
- The Scorpions
- St Mary's
- TCC

Competition Rules

Points

Five points shall be awarded to the winning team.

A batting point shall be awarded for every 30 runs scored.

A bowling point shall be awarded for every two wickets taken.

One-day games

The side batting second shall face the same number of overs as the side bowling first manages to bowl in 90 minutes.

Batters shall retire on making 30 runs.

Retired batters may return to the crease only if all other batters have been dismissed.

Any bowler cannot bowl more than four overs.

Two-day games

The side batting second shall face the same number of overs as the side bowling first manages to bowl in three and a half hours.

Batters shall retire on making 40 runs.

Retired batters may return to the crease only if all other batters have been dismissed.

Any bowler cannot bowl more than eight overs.

Finals

After the five round robin games have been played the following finals will be scheduled.

Semi-finals (venue — home grounds of first-named teams)

Game A Team 1 v Team 4

Game B Team 2 v Team 3

Grand final (venue — highest placed winner from semi-finals)

Winner of Game A v Winner of Game B

Draw

Round 1 (one-dayer)

St Mary's v TCC
Riverwall v Motherwell State
The Scorpions v Benchley Park

Round 2 (two-dayer)

Riverwall v St Mary's
Motherwell State v Benchley Park
TCC v The Scorpions

Round 3 (two-dayer)

Motherwell State v St Mary's
The Scorpions v Riverwall
Benchley Park v TCC

Round 4 (one-dayer)

Riverwall v Benchley Park
The Scorpions v St Mary's
TCC v Motherwell State

Round 5 (two-dayer)

Motherwell State v The Scorpions
TCC v Riverwall
Benchley Park v St Mary's

Semi-finals (two-dayer)

1st v 4th
3rd v 2nd

Grand final (two-dayer)

Two winners of semi-final

Scores and Ladders

ROUND 1

St Mary's 5/112 lost to TCC 4/135
Riverwall 7/164 defeated Motherwell State 107
The Scorpions 5/186 defeated Benchley Park 35 and 68

Points

Win 5 points
30 runs 1 point
2 wickets 1 point

Ladder	P	W	L	Bat P	Bowl P	Win P	Total
The Scorpions	1	1		6	10	5	21
Riverwall	1	1		5	5	5	15
TCC	1	1		4	2	5	11
Motherwell State	1		1	3	3		6
Benchley Park	1		1	3	2		5
St Mary's	1		1	3	2		5

ROUND 2

Riverwall 8/271 defeated St Mary's 160
Motherwell State 8/214 defeated Benchley Park 6/204
TCC 147 lost to The Scorpions 7/283

Ladder	P	W	L	Bat P	Bowl P	Win P	Total
The Scorpions	2	2		15	15	10	40
Riverwall	2	2		14	10	10	34
Motherwell State	2	1	1	10	6	5	21
TCC	2	1	1	8	5	5	18
Benchley Park	2		2	9	6		15
St Mary's	2		2	8	6		14

ROUND 3

Riverwall 9/174 lost to The Scorpions 9/175
Motherwell State 131 lost to St Mary's 8/142
Benchley Park 109 defeated TCC 9/96

Ladder	P	W	L	Bat P	Bowl P	Win P	Total
The Scorpions	3	3		20	19	15	54
Riverwall	3	2	1	19	14	10	43
Motherwell State	3	1	2	14	10	5	29
St Mary's	3	1	2	12	11	5	28
Benchley Park	3	1	2	12	10	5	27
TCC	3	1	2	11	10	5	26

Riverwall Scores and Statistics

	Games	Runs	Highest	Average	Wickets
Jono	3	90	57 no	45	4
Cameron	3	77	33 no	38.5	2
Rahul	3	66	61 no	33	4
Martian	1	7	7 no	7	
Jimbo	0				
Scott	3	45	31 ret	22.5	10
Toby	3	86	32 no	86	4
Gavin	3	38	19	19	
Georgie	3	46	20	15.3	1
Minh	2	18	18	9	
Jay	3	43	17 ret	21.5	
Ally	2	20	19 no	20	
Ahmazru	3	14	11	4.7	
Jason	1	20	20	20	

Game	1	2	3	4	5	S/F	G/F
Jono	33	57 no	0				
Cameron	17	27	33 ret				
Rahul	5	61 no	0				
Scott	31 ret	6	8				
Toby	25 ret	32 ret	29				
Martian	7 no	dnp	dnp				
Jimbo	dnp	dnp	dnp				
Gavin	0	19	19				
Georgie	12	14	20				
Minh	0	18	dnp				
Jay	17 ret	13	13				
Ally	dnp	1	19 no				
Ahmazru	11	3	0				
Jason	dnp	dnp	20				
(extras)	8	20	13				
Totals	7/164	8/271	9/174				

HOW TO PLAY DICE CRICKET

- You will need: dice, paper and pencils, and a friend!
- Each player creates their own team of eleven cricketers, maybe including yourself! You can choose a team from a particular country or an era.
- Each cricketer is given a number of chances before they are given out. The batters in the team have more chances — for example, a great batsman like Steve Waugh might get five chances but a specialist bowler like Glenn McGrath might only get one. Both players must agree on how many chances each cricketer gets, and the total number of chances for each team must be the same. Write the number of chances each cricketer has next to his/her name, and set your batting order.
- Roll the dice to work out the order of play. Whoever rolls the highest number gets to choose whether their team will bat or bowl first.
- Open the innings and roll the dice for the first batter. The number on the dice roll is the number of runs scored, and rolling a one or three also means the batters 'change ends' so that the other batter is on strike.
- If a five is rolled, it is a chance or a wicket. There are no runs scored. If the first roll for a batter is a five, then he/she is out for nothing, regardless of the number of chances available.
- The number eleven player only gets one chance and a maximum three rolls of the dice.
- After a batter is out, roll the dice to see how he/she was dismissed:

1. Bowled	4. lbw
2. Caught	5. Run out
3. Caught	6. Caught and bowled, or stumped – you choose!

- You may like to allocate a number (1-6) to your bowlers to see who takes the wickets. Roll the dice again to work out who dismissed the batter.
- At the end of the innings roll the dice twice each to work out the number of wides and no-balls, and once for byes and leg byes.

GLOSSARY

bails Two small pieces of wood that sit on top of the stumps. At least one has to fall off the stumps for a bowled or run-out decision to be made.

centre-wicket practice Team practice played out on a cricket field, as opposed to in the nets. Sometimes two or more bowlers are used, one after the other, to speed up the practice. If the batter goes out, he or she usually stays on for more batting practice.

covers A fielding position on the side of the wicket that the batter is facing, halfway between the bowler and the wicketkeeper.

crease There are quite a few creases in cricket. They are lines drawn near the stumps that help the batters and bowlers know where they are in relation to the stumps.

fine leg A fielding position down near the boundary line behind the wicket keeper. Often a fast bowler fields in this position.

gully A close-in fielding position along from the slips – the fielders next to the wicket-keeper.

lbw If the bowler hits the pads or a part of the batter's body with the ball, and he or she thinks that the ball would have gone on and hit the stumps (as long as it pitched in line of the stumps), then the bowler can appeal for lbw. If the umpire is sure that the batter didn't hit the ball with the bat, then the batter may be given out. It can get more complicated though!

leg-stump There are three stumps. This is the stump that is nearest the legs of the batter.

maiden If a bowler bowls an over and no runs are scored from it, then it is called a maiden.

mid-off A fielding position next to the bowler. It is on the off, or bat side of the pitch as the batter looks down the wicket.

mid-on A fielding position next to the bowler. It is on the on, or leg side of the pitch as the batter looks down the wicket.

no ball If a bowler puts his or her foot entirely over the return crease (the marked line) then it is a no ball and the batter can't be given out – unless it is a run-out.

off-stump The stump that is on the batting side of the batter. The other stump is the middle stump.

third man A fielding position down behind the wicketkeeper but on the other side of the fine leg fielder. The third man fielder is behind the slips fielders.

yorker The name for a delivery, usually bowled by a medium or fast bowler, that is pitched right up near the batter's feet. It is full pitched and fast.

About the Authors

MICHAEL PANCKRIDGE has worked as a teacher for more than 15 years. He has been a lifelong fan of all sports, especially cricket. Michael has both played and coached cricket but is quite sure he has never clocked a speed at even half the pace that Brett Lee bowls at. Michael lives in Geelong with his wife Jo and daughters Eliza and Bronte.

BRETT LEE grew up in Wollongong, New South Wales, and is the younger brother of former international cricketing all-rounder Shane Lee. Brett made his first-class cricketing debut in 1995 and his Australian debut against India in 1999/2000. He is one of the country's fastest ever bowlers, regularly clocking speeds of over 150 kilometres per hour.